FROM THE NANCY DREW FILES

THE CASE: *Nancy's investigation of a car theft takes a sharp and dangerous turn—into corruption and murder!*

CONTACT: *The theft of Bess's new yellow Camaro gives her the blues and gives Nancy a line on a deadly case of criminal conspiracy.*

SUSPECTS: Dirk Walters—*At the track he lives in the fast lane. On the side he may be playing fast and loose with the law.*

Kitty Lambert—*She's the hottest mechanic on the circuit, and she has all the tools to hot-wire a car.*

The police Auto Theft Unit—*Vanishing leads and destroyed evidence could mean that one bad cop is driving the investigation into the ground.*

COMPLICATIONS: *Bess has agreed to go out on a date with Dirk—the man who may have masterminded the theft of her car and the murder of his own mechanic!*

Books in The Nancy Drew Files® Series

#1 SECRETS CAN KILL
#2 DEADLY INTENT
#3 MURDER ON ICE
#4 SMILE AND SAY MURDER
#5 HIT AND RUN HOLIDAY
#6 WHITE WATER TERROR
#7 DEADLY DOUBLES
#8 TWO POINTS TO MURDER
#9 FALSE MOVES
#10 BURIED SECRETS
#11 HEART OF DANGER
#12 FATAL RANSOM
#13 WINGS OF FEAR
#14 THIS SIDE OF EVIL
#15 TRIAL BY FIRE
#16 NEVER SAY DIE
#17 STAY TUNED FOR DANGER
#18 CIRCLE OF EVIL
#19 SISTERS IN CRIME
#20 VERY DEADLY YOURS
#21 RECIPE FOR MURDER
#22 FATAL ATTRACTION
#23 SINISTER PARADISE
#24 TILL DEATH DO US PART
#25 RICH AND DANGEROUS
#26 PLAYING WITH FIRE
#27 MOST LIKELY TO DIE
#28 THE BLACK WIDOW
#29 PURE POISON
#30 DEATH BY DESIGN
#31 TROUBLE IN TAHITI
#32 HIGH MARKS FOR MALICE
#33 DANGER IN DISGUISE
#34 VANISHING ACT
#35 BAD MEDICINE
#36 OVER THE EDGE
#37 LAST DANCE
#38 THE FINAL SCENE
#39 THE SUSPECT NEXT DOOR
#40 SHADOW OF A DOUBT
#41 SOMETHING TO HIDE
#42 THE WRONG CHEMISTRY
#43 FALSE IMPRESSIONS
#44 SCENT OF DANGER
#45 OUT OF BOUNDS
#46 WIN, PLACE OR DIE
#47 FLIRTING WITH DANGER
#48 A DATE WITH DECEPTION
#49 PORTRAIT IN CRIME
#50 DEEP SECRETS
#51 A MODEL CRIME
#52 DANGER FOR HIRE
#53 TRAIL OF LIES
#54 COLD AS ICE
#55 DON'T LOOK TWICE
#56 MAKE NO MISTAKE
#57 INTO THIN AIR
#58 HOT PURSUIT
#59 HIGH RISK
#60 POISON PEN
#61 SWEET REVENGE
#62 EASY MARKS
#63 MIXED SIGNALS
#64 THE WRONG TRACK
#65 FINAL NOTES
#66 TALL, DARK AND DEADLY
#67 NOBODY'S BUSINESS
#68 CROSSCURRENTS
#69 RUNNING SCARED
#70 CUTTING EDGE
#71 HOT TRACKS

THE NANCY DREW FILES™

Case 71
HOT TRACKS

CAROLYN KEENE

AN ARCHWAY PAPERBACK
Published by POCKET BOOKS
New York London Toronto Sydney Tokyo Singapore

AN ARCHWAY PAPERBACK *Original*

An Archway Paperback published by
POCKET BOOKS, a division of Simon & Schuster Inc.
1230 Avenue of the Americas, New York, NY 10020

Produced by Mega-Books of New York, Inc.

ISBN: 0-671-73075-4

First Archway Paperback printing May 1992

10 9 8 7 6 5 4 3 2 1

Cover art by Tricia Zimic

Printed in the U.S.A.

IL 6+

Chapter One

"Wow, what a great car!" Nancy Drew exclaimed. She ran her fingers along the shiny hood of the yellow Camaro, then stood back to inspect the sports car.

"After a full year of saving up, it's all mine," Bess Marvin said proudly. With a big grin, she held up the keys and jingled them. "Ready for a ride?"

Nancy's blue eyes sparkled with anticipation. "Definitely!" She had driven Bess over to the used car lot to pick up the Camaro. Now the papers were all signed, and Bess was free to drive the car away.

While Bess opened the driver's door, Nancy jogged around to the passenger side and climbed in. "Nice seats," she said. "They're comfortable, and the color is—" She had spoken before she really looked. The seat covers and carpet were an ugly brown, but she didn't want to burst Bess's bubble.

"I know. The color's gross." Bess plucked at the sleeve of her red jumpsuit. "My dream car would've been candy apple red with white leather seats. But the dealer said he doesn't get many used Camaros, and I could never afford a new one. I was so excited when he called about this one that I didn't even care about the seats. To me it's the most beautiful car in the world!"

Nancy patted the dashboard. "It is really nice," she agreed. "George is going to die when she sees it. It's too bad she couldn't come today."

"I understand, though," Bess said with a shrug. "I mean, if I had a choice between sailing with my boyfriend's family and going to a car dealership, I'd choose the guy any time."

Bess's cousin George Fayne usually did everything with Nancy and Bess. This time, though, she had chosen to go sailing with Kevin Davis, her new boyfriend, and his family for five days.

"So let's get going," Bess went on. She turned the key in the ignition, and the motor jumped to life with a powerful roar.

"All right!" Nancy said. "The next time somebody leads us on a high-speed chase we're taking this baby."

Bess whisked her blond hair behind her ears and playfully poked Nancy on the arm. "Are you ready for the ride of your life?"

Nancy checked her watch. "You're not going to believe this, but we don't have time for a ride," she told Bess. "I made our dinner reservations for six-thirty, and I hear the Riverside gives them away if you're late. I'd better just take my car and meet you there." Stepping out of the Camaro, Nancy smoothed her cotton sweater and short denim skirt.

"See you there," Bess said, leaning across the seat to speak to Nancy.

After climbing into her blue Mustang, Nancy took a second to comb her reddish blond hair and check her lipstick in the rearview mirror. A squeal of tires made her look out the window in time to see the Camaro buck. It came to a complete stop before Bess restarted the engine and pulled out of the lot. Having Bess behind the wheel of her own car was going to be a real adventure!

Nancy started the Mustang and headed after her friend. She didn't catch another glimpse of the yellow Camaro until she pulled into the parking lot of the Riverside.

The restaurant was located in a recently renovated area along the Muskoka River. The Scene, a new nightclub, was next to it, and several boutiques and smaller restaurants had opened up along the narrow winding road that led down from the highway. The whole area was bathed in a warm glow.

As Nancy pulled into the restaurant parking lot, she saw that Bess had found a parking space right beside the front entrance, between a Mercedes and a BMW.

"Look at this, Nan," Bess yelled through her open window. "VIP parking!"

With a wave, Nancy drove the Mustang around the crowded lot. Finally she found an empty spot under a willow tree at the side of the building. After she walked around to the front of the restaurant, she noticed that the door of the Camaro was open. There was no sign of Bess.

"Bess?" Nancy called, feeling a sudden twinge of nervousness.

"In here!"

Nancy stepped up close to the car. Bess was bent low in the driver's seat, searching for something on the floor.

"My purse fell, and all my junk spilled out." Bess moaned.

Nancy laughed. "No wonder! You jerked out of the car dealer's."

"Did not. I only stalled out once. Oh no! The top of my perfume bottle just came off. The carpet's getting soaked." Bess sat up, holding her nose. "Now the whole car stinks."

With a teasing smile, Nancy said, "At least now you and your car smell the same."

"True," Bess said brightly. "Besides, I can't do anything about it now, so let's eat. I hear the Riverside has the best seafood. Though it's too bad we didn't decide on carryout." She patted the top of the car before shutting and locking the door. "I hate to leave this baby for even a second."

"Your car will be fine," Nancy assured her. She linked her arm through Bess's, and the two girls walked to the stone steps. The Riverside was built to resemble the quaint buildings in the seaside towns of Maine. It had a wood-shingled roof, weathered natural wood siding, and white shutters.

"It looks crowded," Nancy commented as she opened the screen door and they stepped inside. "It's a good thing we made reservations."

Ten minutes later the girls were seated at a small table on the back porch of the restaurant. A huge glass window wrapped around the porch.

"What a view!" Bess exclaimed, glancing out at the sun as it glinted behind a row of willows on the steep bank of the river. Deep golden reflections streaked the water's surface. "It's amazing to think that's the same muddy river we cross over every day on the highway."

"Really," Nancy agreed. "It looks so wild, I feel as if I really am in Maine."

"Mmm. Maine. That reminds me of lobster, my favorite," Bess said, scanning the menu.

Nancy picked up her menu and began studying it, too. "Shrimp sounds good to me."

"*Ssst.* Nancy," Bess hissed a few moments

later. When Nancy raised her eyes, her friend was peering at her around the side of the menu.

"What?"

Bess nodded her head to the right. "Look at that guy, four tables over," she whispered.

Nancy glanced casually over. A cute guy about their age was just being seated. "What about him?" she asked Bess in a low voice.

"He went to high school with us. I think his name is Dirk Walters. Do you remember him?"

Nancy stared at the guy again. He was leaning forward in his chair, studying his menu. His sun-streaked sandy hair was cropped short, and his arms and face were tanned a golden brown.

"Sort of," Nancy replied, turning back to Bess. "I'm not surprised that *you* remember, though. You never forget a cute guy."

"That's for sure! And Dirk was the cutest in my English class." She frowned slightly and added, "The trouble was, he was only interested in cars."

"May I take your order?" the waitress asked, interrupting the girls.

"I'll have the lobster tail," Bess said promptly, "to celebrate owning my first car."

Nancy ordered the fried shrimp. After the waitress left, she glanced back at Dirk Walters. He was sipping a soda, staring at them. Suddenly he stood up and strode directly over to their table.

"You're Bess, right?" he asked, curiosity lighting up his green eyes. "Bess Marvin from English class."

Bess flashed him her brightest smile. "Right, and you're Dirk Walters. How are you?"

"Great!" Dirk pulled out an extra chair, twirled it around and straddled it backward. "How about you?"

"Fantastic. Do you remember Nancy Drew?" Bess added. "She was in our grade, too."

"Drew, Drew—" Dirk furrowed his brow as he mulled over the name. "You were in my algebra class in tenth grade."

"I was?" Nancy asked, surprised that he remembered.

"Yeah. Straight As as I recall." Dirk laughed, then turned back to Bess, who was blushing slightly as she beamed at him.

Nancy rolled her eyes. She knew her friend well enough to know what *that* smile meant. Bess was getting another of her instant crushes. Not that Nancy could blame her. If it weren't for Ned Nickerson, Nancy's steady boyfriend, she might have been just as interested. Dirk Walters was definitely a hunk.

Nancy listened idly as Dirk explained what he had been doing since they had graduated high school.

"I've been crewing for a guy who's on the drag-racing circuit," he was saying. "We've been all over the state this year."

"Drag racing!" Bess exclaimed. "I should've

guessed. You always had a car magazine stuck in your English book."

Just then the waitress came with the girls' salads. Dirk reluctantly stood up.

"Well, I guess I'd better let you eat," he said. "Hey, why don't you come out to the racetrack Friday at about two? I'll get you passes into the pit area. I'm racing this weekend, and again in next weekend's Memorial Day race. It's kind of a big deal for me—it's the first time I'll be running my own car."

"That sounds neat. We'd love to!" Bess gushed.

Nancy gulped down a tomato. Neat? She couldn't believe Bess was so excited about the prospect of spending time at a hot, smelly, noisy racetrack. This crush on Dirk Walters must be serious!

"Great," said Dirk. "I'll call you with the details." Bess found a pen in her purse, and he wrote her phone number down on the back of his hand. Then, with a wave, he went back to his table.

Bess gave a dreamy sigh. "He's more gorgeous than ever. Nancy, I think I'm in love!"

"From the way Dirk stared at you, I'd say it's mutual," Nancy said.

"Do you really think so?" Bess asked.

Nancy nodded. Just then the waitress came with their main course. Pointing at Bess's untouched salad, Nancy said, "You'd better eat before love makes you wither away to nothing."

"I'm too excited," Bess declared, picking up her fork. "Though I must say this lobster looks yummy, and—"

Abruptly, she stopped talking. Nancy saw that Bess had focused her attention on Dirk's table, her fork frozen in midair.

Nancy followed Bess's gaze in time to see a tall, lithe brunette greet Dirk with a hug and sit down at his table. Dirk motioned to the waitress, then leaned forward and began talking to the brunette, an eager expression on his face.

"I don't believe it!" Bess said, frowning. She angrily speared her lobster tail with her fork. "He had a date with another girl!"

"Maybe it's not a *date* date," Nancy said, trying to reassure her friend.

"Well, I know one thing—they're not discussing gear shifts!" She cut off a piece of lobster, swirled it in butter sauce, and popped it into her mouth.

Immediately her expression brightened. "I know another thing, too," she added. "No guy's going to ruin my dinner. This lobster is delicious. Let's enjoy our food, and as soon as we leave, Dirk Walters will be history."

Forty-five minutes later the girls had paid their bill and were getting up to leave. Through the whole meal, Dirk and his friend had chatted animatedly. Only when the attractive brunette had left the table for several minutes did Dirk look over and smile at Bess.

On their way out, Bess purposefully led them right past Dirk's table. Nancy overheard Dirk say to the brunette, "It's a date, then. I'll see you Friday." He raised his eyes to Bess and Nancy.

" 'Bye, Dirk," Bess said coolly before stalking out of the restaurant.

Nancy caught up with her outside on the porch. Even in the dark, she could see that Bess was fuming.

"Do you believe the nerve of that jerk?" Bess asked, her hands on her hips. "He asked *us* to the races on Friday, too. Who does he think he is?"

"Just be glad you found out about the guy *before* you started dating him."

Bess let out a long breath of air. "You're right," she agreed. "I hope the Camaro didn't miss me too much. Come on, I'll race the Mustang home."

The two girls started down the restaurant steps. Except for a few pockets of light from outside lamps, the parking lot was dark with menacing shadows.

"Let's still go to the races Friday afternoon," Bess suggested, pausing halfway down the steps. "It'll be fun to see how Romeo Walters handles three dates."

She began giggling. A moment later the

laughter died on her lips. She was staring straight ahead, her eyes wide with horror.

"What is it?" Nancy asked. Then she noticed that the parking space between the Mercedes and BMW was empty.

"Nancy!" Bess gasped. "The Camaro's gone!"

Chapter Two

BESS HURRIED over to the empty spot. "Didn't I park my car right here?" she asked frantically.

"You sure did," Nancy said, frowning. The sparkle of something shining on the ground near Bess caught her eye. After striding up to it, Nancy stooped down to get a closer look.

Pieces of shattered safety glass were scattered along the asphalt near the empty parking spot. "This looks like it's from a car window," she told Bess, holding a piece up to the light. "It's about the right thickness."

Bess didn't seem to have heard Nancy. "Maybe I made a mistake," she said, glancing around the parking lot. "Maybe I parked it over there."

She began to walk to the next row. Nancy jumped up and caught her arm.

"This is where you parked it," Nancy said gently. "It looks as if somebody broke into your car and stole it."

Bess whirled around to stare at Nancy. "Stole it! No. No way." She shook her head in disbelief. "Maybe someone from the restaurant moved it. Or it was towed away because—because it was in a no parking zone. Or—or—"

"Bess," Nancy cut in, "I'll help you look around if it'll make you feel better, but I'm afraid your Camaro's gone. It looks as if someone broke the window and unlocked the car."

Tears welled up in Bess's eyes, and Nancy's heart went out to her friend. "Come on. Let's make a quick search of the parking lot," she suggested. "Then we'll call the police."

Bess nodded. The two girls checked out all the rows of cars in front of the restaurant, then walked around to the side. Nancy's Mustang was still under the willow tree, but there was no sign of the yellow Camaro.

"Maybe someone in the restaurant knows something," Bess said hopefully.

Inside, the hostess directed Nancy and Bess to the manager's office. The hostess hadn't seen anything unusual, and Nancy doubted that any of the people eating had, either. None of the tables had a view of the parking lot.

"We'd better call the police," the manager advised after Nancy and Bess told him what had happened. "Yours is the third car this week that's been stolen from the area." He gestured to the telephone on his desk. "Here. You can use my phone."

"I can't believe this is happening," Bess groaned, slumping down into the chair in front of the desk. She dialed the River Heights police station. When the dispatcher answered, Bess gave her name and explained when and where the car had been stolen.

"A patrol car will be right here," she told Nancy after she'd hung up. With a sigh, she added, "I'd better call my parents, too."

Nancy nodded. "I'll wait for you outside. I want to look around."

After making her way back out of the restaurant, Nancy pulled her pocket flashlight from her purse and hunted around the empty parking spot for any clue as to what had happened to the Camaro. Except for the shards of glass, there was nothing unusual.

Bess came down the stairs just as Nancy finished her search. She sat dejectedly on the bottom step with her chin cupped in her hands.

"What did your dad say?" Nancy asked, flicking off her light and sitting down next to Bess.

"He was speechless. Not that I blame him. I mean, just this afternoon he was cosigning for my car loan, and now it's gone! I just can't figure out why anyone took it. Why not steal the BMW or Mercedes? They're worth a lot more."

Nancy shrugged. "I don't know much about auto theft. Maybe the police can tell us why." She nodded toward the entrance of the parking lot, where a white cruiser was just pulling in.

The police car stopped next to Nancy and Bess, and a young officer climbed out. "Hi. I'm Officer Jackson," she said. "Are you the people who called about the stolen car?"

"Yes. I'm Nancy Drew, and this is Bess Marvin," Nancy said. She and Bess stood and shook hands with the police officer.

"It was my Camaro," Bess added.

"Where was it parked?" Officer Jackson asked.

Nancy pointed to the empty space, and the policewoman bent down to examine the glass.

"What I can't understand is how they started the car without the keys," Bess said.

Officer Jackson stood up, took a pad from her shirt pocket, and flipped it open. "They probably hot-wired it," she told Bess. "All a person needs is a tool to pull out the ignition system. Then he jams a screwdriver in, twists it, and your car starts. It only takes a professional about a minute."

With a nod at Bess, the officer added, "Now, let me get some information from you, Ms. Marvin. Then I can broadcast the car's description over the radio."

As Bess walked over to the cruiser with

Officer Jackson, Nancy went over in her mind what had happened. They'd been in the restaurant about an hour and a half, but it wasn't dark except for the last few minutes. Chances were that the thief had driven away in the Camaro just minutes before she and Bess had come outside.

With a frustrated sigh, Nancy joined Bess and Officer Jackson at the police cruiser.

"I'm also calling the description in to the National Crime Information Center," the officer was telling Bess. "They'll put it into the computer. That way the Camaro can be traced as a stolen car anywhere in the United States."

"What a day," Bess said glumly while Officer Jackson slid into the cruiser to broadcast her report. "First Dirk, and now this."

"Bess," a male voice said behind them. "What's going on? Are you all right?"

Nancy and Bess turned to see Dirk Walters coming down the restaurant stairs. The brunette was right beside him. Dirk hopped down the last three steps and came to stand in front of Bess.

"Why the cop?" he asked. "Is something wrong?"

"My car was stolen," Bess told him.

"Stolen! Are you sure?"

Nancy nodded. "We checked the entire lot," she told him. "Plus the manager told us it wasn't the first one that's been stolen from this area."

Dirk gave a low whistle. "That's awful."

"Awful doesn't begin to describe it," Bess said. "It was brand-new! At least to me. My first car." Her lower lip began to tremble.

Dirk took her hand. "Hey, cheer up. I bet a couple of kids just 'borrowed' it for a joyride. The cops will probably find it across town."

"Uh, Dirk, I have to go," the brunette suddenly said. She was still standing on the steps.

Nancy noticed that the woman was a little older than they were—maybe in her mid-twenties—and very attractive. Her face was already tan and was carefully made up, and she wore a rose-colored silk dress with a soft, flowing skirt. Nancy detected a hardness in the woman's brown eyes, and frown lines had already formed on her brow.

"Oh, sorry." Dirk sprang back up the stairs. Taking the woman's elbow, he escorted her over to Nancy and Bess. "Kitty Lambert, this is Bess Marvin and Nancy Drew. I went to high school with them."

"Nice to meet you," Nancy said.

Bess gave Kitty a forced smile. She wasn't happy about meeting Dirk's date.

"Kitty's going to crew for me the next couple of races," Dirk said enthusiastically. "Isn't that great?"

"Yeah, great," Bess echoed flatly. She was curiously eyeing the brunette.

Kitty gave them a polite smile. "Nice meeting you, but I have to run. Sorry about your car, Bess. See you Friday, Dirk," she called over her shoulder. She walked quickly across the parking lot to a white Firebird and got in.

Dirk waved as Kitty drove away, then turned to grin at Nancy and Bess. "Imagine, Kitty Lambert, the best mechanic around, crewing for me."

"She's a mechanic?" Bess asked.

Dirk nodded. "The best. I'm still not sure why she agreed to work for *me.* Lots of the hotshot drivers want her. The only thing I can figure is that she's got a thing for my older brother, Jake."

Bess shot Nancy a relieved look. "Or maybe she figures you'll be the next Grand Prix champion," she suggested brightly.

Dirk chuckled. "Actually, that's a different kind of racing from drag racing."

"Sounds like I have a lot to learn," Bess added. She opened her mouth to say something else but stopped when Officer Jackson came over.

"The report is in, so all the patrol cars in the area will be notified," the officer told them. "The auto theft unit will contact you as soon as they learn anything. In the meantime, make sure you call your insurance company."

"Do you two need a ride home?" Dirk asked.

"Thanks, but I have my car here," Nancy replied.

"Then I'd better be going." Turning to Bess,

he asked, "Walk me to my car a second? It's right over there."

As they walked away, Nancy said to Officer Jackson, "The manager told us that some other cars were stolen from this area recently."

The policewoman nodded, putting her pad back into her shirt pocket. "Two others to be exact. They were taken from the main parking lot across the street last weekend. We've stepped up our patrols, but the thieves have eluded us so far."

"But why this riverfront area?" Nancy asked.

"Who knows?" Officer Jackson shrugged. "My guess is that most of the people who are attracted to the nightclub and restaurants here are young people, and young people generally like sporty cars. The thieves know the owners will be inside dancing and eating so they'll have plenty of time to break in and steal a car. Plus, this lot isn't very well lighted. We've already spoken to the owners about the problem. They've agreed to do something about it, but it'll take a while."

Bess rejoined them, a faint smile on her face, and Nancy couldn't help smiling, too. Obviously, the budding romance with Dirk was back on track.

"Officer Jackson was telling me about the other thefts in the area," Nancy explained to Bess.

"So what are the odds of finding my car?" Bess asked.

"Oh, the odds are good," Officer Jackson told her. "About ninety percent of all stolen cars are recovered."

"That's terrific!" Bess exclaimed.

"Well, not so terrific." The policewoman became very serious. "Usually by the time the cars are found, they've either been burned, wrecked, or are in pieces."

Chapter Three

"You mean I may never see my Camaro in one piece again?" Bess asked, her face falling.

Officer Jackson nodded. "Unfortunately. If it was stolen by a professional, your car's probably in a chop shop by now."

Seeing Bess's confused expression, the officer went on to explain. "A chop shop is where a thief can get rid of a stolen car. The shops dismantle the cars or repaint them. Then they resell them whole or as parts."

"Don't tell me any more," Bess groaned and covered her ears. "It's all too awful!"

Officer Jackson smiled sympathetically. "Well, I've got to go," she said. "Call the station if you have any questions or want to check on the progress of the investigation. Ask for Detective Quinones. He's in charge of auto theft."

The girls thanked the police officer. After the cruiser had driven away, Nancy turned to Bess.

"Come on. While you're standing there, some kid could be joyriding in your car. If we leave now, we may even catch him."

Bess's outlook brightened. "You think so?"

"Well, there's always a chance."

"Then let's go!" Bess grabbed Nancy's arm and pulled her toward the side lot where the Mustang was parked. "Just wait till I get hold of the creep who stole my car," she said angrily. "I'll—"

"Call the police?" Nancy suggested.

Bess giggled. "Probably."

Nancy unlocked the car doors, and she and Bess slid in. "So did you and Dirk make up?" Nancy asked.

"Yeah. In fact, he invited me to lunch tomorrow. I think he knew I was a little bent out of shape about Kitty." Bess's smile faded as she added, "But believe it or not, my mind's not on Dirk right now. I only want to find my car."

Nancy drove out of the parking lot and up the winding road away from the river to the main highway. After rolling down the window, she propped her elbow on the door. Warm spring air blew into the car and ruffled her reddish blond hair.

"Let's think. If you were a kid joyriding in a

hot Camaro, where would you go?" she wondered.

"I'd head straight for the action," Bess said without hesitating.

"And where's the action in River Heights?" Nancy asked Bess.

"The mall!" they chorused together.

"So let's try there first. We're only about five minutes away," said Nancy. She checked her watch. "It's nine. The mall closes at nine-thirty, so the parking lot should be starting to thin out."

Bess crossed her fingers. "Let's hope whoever took my car just left it there."

"Yeah, let's hope." Nancy was glad they had decided to search for the Camaro. It was better than doing nothing, and it seemed to have lifted Bess's spirits. Deep down, Nancy knew the chances of finding the car were pretty slim, but she just didn't have the heart to tell Bess.

As Nancy pulled the Mustang into the mall's huge parking lot, Bess rolled down her window and stuck her head out. The two girls scanned the cars as they cruised slowly up and down each row.

Twenty minutes later Bess let out a breath in a loud sigh of frustration. "This is crazy," she grumbled. "My neck's got a kink in it, and there's no sign of my car. I think we're on a wild-goose chase."

"Do you want to give up?" Nancy asked.

"No. It's just that— Hey, look over there!"

Bess straightened up and pointed out the front window of the Mustang. A yellow Camaro was backing out of a parking space.

"Hold on!" Nancy said, stepping on the gas.

The Camaro started to pull forward just as Nancy swung her car around, blocking its path. She then stomped on the brakes. The car had barely stopped before Bess opened her door and jumped out.

"Bess!" Nancy called, throwing open her own door. "Be careful. The person could be dangerous!"

Her warning came too late. In two strides, Bess had already reached the driver's side of the Camaro.

Nancy raced after her—then did a quick double take as the window on the Camaro was slowly cranked down. A white-haired woman was in the driver's seat. Not only that, but the Camaro's interior was blue instead of brown.

"Is something the matter?" the elderly woman asked in a quavering voice. There was a puzzled expression on her wrinkled face.

"Uh . . ." Bess stammered. "We're looking for— It's just that—"

"My friend thought you were her grandmother," Nancy fibbed. "Sorry—our mistake."

The woman nodded. "That's all right." She waved cheerfully before putting the car in reverse and stepping on the gas. With a squeal of the tires, the Camaro whipped back into an empty parking space. Nancy and Bess jumped out of the way as the Camaro lurched forward again, narrowly missing them before it sped down the aisle away from the Mustang.

"See the way she's driving?" Bess sputtered. "She can't be an elderly lady. She's a thief in disguise—and you're letting her get away!"

Nancy laughed. "Relax. That wasn't your car. It had blue seats. Plus the window wasn't broken."

"I knew that," Bess retorted with an embarrassed laugh. "I just got carried away."

"Next time be a little more cautious before charging up to a car," Nancy said as they climbed back into the Mustang. "If that had been the kid who stole your car, he might've been dangerous."

Bess nodded thoughtfully. "I didn't think about that. You're right. Well, where should we go now?"

Nancy started the Mustang again and headed down the last row of the parking lot. "I hate to say it, but how about home? It's getting late, and I'm kind of beat."

Seeing Bess's disappointed expression, Nancy quickly added, "Not that I'm giving up or anything. It's just that—"

"There's no way we're going to find my car," Bess finished dejectedly.

"It is pretty unlikely," Nancy admitted. "How about if we check out the Loft and Commotion on the way home?" she suggested, hoping to cheer Bess up. "They're hot high-school hangouts. Maybe a kid took your car so he could party at one of those places."

Nancy pulled out of the parking lot and headed for Commotion. She stopped at the first traffic light just as it was turning red. A yellow car waiting on the right side for the light to turn green caught her eye. It was a yellow Camaro.

Nancy nudged her friend. "Look. Check out the plates when it passes by us."

Bess leaned forward as the Camaro drove under the traffic light and continued straight. Nancy and Bess couldn't read the faint tags, but they could tell that they were black and white, like Bess's dealer plates.

"That's got to be my car!" Bess said excitedly.

Nancy's light turned green, and she flipped on her left turn signal. "Let's follow it." She made a sharp turn and almost caught up to the Camaro. There was a light blue sedan between the two cars.

"We've got to get beside it, to see if the window's broken," Bess said determinedly.

"Maybe you can see what color the seat covers are," Nancy added.

Just then the light blue sedan turned off the road. Nancy sped up until she was right behind the Camaro. Then she glanced into the left lane of the two-lane road.

"There are no cars coming," she told Bess.

"I'm going to pull up beside the Camaro. You check it out—but do it quickly!"

Stepping harder on the gas pedal, Nancy shot into the left lane and zoomed up next to the Camaro. Bess stuck her head out the open window. Nancy looked over just in time to see the driver turn his head and stare at them in surprise. He was a guy about their age, with red hair pulled back in a ponytail.

"Mud brown! That's my car!" Bess called out.

At the exact same time the Camaro's motor gave a loud roar, and the car burst ahead of them. Nancy angled back into the right lane and tried to keep up with the yellow sports car.

"The dashboard and seats were definitely brown," Bess said excitedly. "I couldn't tell about the window. It was rolled down."

"That guy wasn't too pleased that we were interested in him, either," Nancy added, her eyes still on the car up ahead. "Let's keep following and find out where he's headed."

Just then the Camaro did a quick U-turn, its tires squealing as the rear end fishtailed.

"Hey, careful with my car!" Bess yelled out the window. Then she steadied herself against the dashboard as Nancy cut the wheel hard to the left.

"Hold on!" Nancy shouted, swinging the Mustang around. "I don't want to lose him."

She could see the yellow Camaro about a quarter mile ahead. Fortunately, there wasn't any traffic, so Nancy went the speed limit trying to catch up to the yellow Camaro.

Soon they were driving into an area with which they weren't very familiar. Large warehouses loomed over the dark streets, which were illuminated only by an occasional street lamp.

"Where are we?" Bess asked worriedly.

"The industrial section of town," Nancy replied. "Lock your door."

Up ahead, the Camaro made an abrupt right turn. Nancy flicked on her blinker and wheeled the Mustang after it.

"Nancy, look." Bess pointed to a sign as they turned the corner. "It's a dead end. We've got him now!"

Nancy's heart sank a moment later. She could see to the end of the street, but the Camaro was nowhere in sight.

Slowing her Mustang, Nancy cruised down the street. Both sides were lined with huge warehouses with loading docks jutting off them. Stacks of empty crates and boxes were piled high against the walls of several of the buildings. Except for two large tractor trailers parked beside one ramp, the area was empty of cars and trucks.

At the end of the street, which was bordered by a chain-link fence, Nancy turned the Mustang around and stopped.

"I don't get it," Bess said, gazing back the way they had come. "Where'd my car go?"

"I don't know. There aren't any alleys or side streets, and it certainly looks as if everything's closed for the night." Nancy shook her head in frustration. "If I didn't know better, I'd say your car disappeared into thin air!"

Chapter Four

"How could my car just disappear?" Bess asked.

Nancy thoughtfully studied the rows of dark warehouses. "I bet the driver pulled into one of these buildings."

"He disappeared so fast, though," Bess said.

"Which means he knew exactly where he was going and the door must have been open," Nancy guessed.

Bess's blue eyes widened as she realized what Nancy was getting at. "You think the chop shop is in one of these buildings?"

"Could be. The question is, which one?"

"Well, we'll just search them all and find out," Bess said firmly. She opened the car door, but Nancy caught her arm and pulled her back.

"Not so fast. Auto theft is big business, Bess. If anyone catches us snooping around, we might find ourselves in a whole lot of trouble."

Shivering, Bess closed and relocked the car door. "So now what?"

Nancy stepped on the gas and began driving back down the dead-end street. "We find out exactly where we are now, then call the police," she told Bess.

The girls didn't see any street signs at the intersection. "We can use the Pacific Trucking Company and Illinois Overseas signs as landmarks," Nancy suggested, pointing to the buildings on either side of the intersection. She turned left, heading back the way they'd come.

"Look. That street sign says Twelfth, and there's Fourteenth," Bess added. "So the dead end must be about Tenth."

They drove until they were once again on the main highway, busy with late-night traffic. At a well-lit gas station, Nancy spotted a phone booth. They parked next to it and got out of the car.

"Let's hope they'll let us speak to someone in auto theft," Nancy said, dialing the River Heights police. She told the dispatcher that she had some information about a stolen car and asked to speak to Detective Quinones, the man Officer Jackson had said was in charge of auto theft.

The dispatcher told her that the detective wasn't available and instructed her to come in first thing in the morning to file a report.

"In the morning!" Bess wailed after Nancy hung up. "By then my car will be in a hundred pieces!"

"Maybe not." Nancy tried to reassure her. "It's late, and all those warehouses seemed deserted. Probably the guy with the red pony-tail just drops off the cars he steals at night. The Camaro might not get worked on until tomorrow."

"Let's hope so," Bess said, "because I'll be furious if all they recover tomorrow is my ugly brown dashboard!"

"This is the office of the auto theft unit?" Bess whispered dubiously to Nancy the next morning. The two girls had paused outside a small, dingy room on the top floor of the River Heights police station.

"This is where the desk clerk sent us," Nancy said, glancing around as they stepped inside.

The room was divided into two cubicles. Two desks piled with papers were jammed into the cubicle closest to the door. The other cubicle had a desk with a computer and printer and a rubber plant with three dusty leaves.

"Can I help you girls?" a man's voice said from the hall behind Nancy and Bess.

Nancy whirled around to see a paunchy, middle-aged guy in a rumpled tweed sports jacket, holding a jelly doughnut.

"Uh, yes," Nancy said. She introduced herself and Bess, then asked, "Is this auto theft?"

The man waved his doughnut around the room's two cubicles. "This is it." He walked past the girls, taking a bite of the doughnut as he passed. "Now, what can I do for you?" he asked, sitting at one of the two desks in the room's outer cubicle. "I'm Detective Stan Powderly."

"My Camaro was stolen last night," Bess began.

"Camaro, Camaro . . ." Detective Powderly muttered. Setting his doughnut down, he rif-fled through the papers on his desk.

Nancy turned as a younger man wearing cowboy boots and jeans strode into the room, a worn leather jacket draped over one shoul-der. His dark hair was trimmed short around his ears but grew long in the back.

"Hey, Hawk, you know anything about a Camaro?" Detective Powderly asked the new-comer.

The younger guy introduced himself to the girls as Detective B. D. Hawkins. He took a folder from the second desk and opened it. "Right here. Jackson took the report," he said in response to Detective Powderly's question. He turned to Nancy with penetrating brown eyes. "Are you Ms. Marvin?"

Nancy pointed at Bess. "No, it was her car."

B.D. chuckled as he skimmed the report. "Not for long, I see," he said. "This must be the shortest ownership on record."

Nancy was amazed at his attitude. He

wasn't being very sympathetic to Bess's predicament.

"Don't mind Detective Hawkins's sense of humor," the older detective said quickly. "He and I are only on temporary assignment in auto theft. Just since this ring of car thieves has been operating. Usually we work in homicide. Chasing cars seems tame compared to murder."

Detective Hawkins smiled apologetically at Bess. "Why don't you tell us what's on your mind."

Nancy looked up as a small, well-built man strode briskly into the room. He had jet black hair, and his dark eyes seemed to snap at the other two men. Powderly wiped sugar off his mouth, and Hawkins slid off his perch on the desk to stand straight.

"Good morning, Stan, B.D." With a frown, the newly arrived man plucked the folder from Detective Hawkins's hands and flipped through it. "Is this Jackson's report?"

"Right," Hawkins said. "This is Bess Marvin and Nancy Drew. Ms. Marvin is the owner of the car."

The dark-haired man nodded at the girls. "I'm Raul Quinones, the detective in charge of auto theft. Ms. Marvin, why don't you go over the report with Detective Powderly to see if there's anything you want to add."

Dropping the folder on the desk, he walked past them and into the cubicle with the computer.

Nancy followed him. "May I speak to you?"

"Go right ahead." With a nod, Detective Quinones began to leaf through a stack of papers.

"After the car was stolen, we drove around town looking for it. We think we spotted it," Nancy began.

"Hmmm," Raul Quinones muttered. He sat down and turned on his computer.

Nancy wondered if he was even listening. Frustrated, she put her hands on the desk and leaned over the top of the computer. "We followed the Camaro until it disappeared down a dead-end street. I think the driver drove it right into a warehouse."

Raul Quinones raised his head sharply to her. "A warehouse? You're sure?"

"Detective Quinones, I'm an experienced detective. I would have noticed if there was any other way out."

"Detective, huh." Quinones seemed to think about it for a second. Then he got up and peered around the partition into the other cubicle. "Stan, B.D. Get in here," he ordered. "Ms. Marvin, you'd better join us, too."

After everyone had squeezed into Quinones's office, Nancy and Bess told the detectives in detail about chasing the yellow Camaro. Nancy noticed that Quinones's face was crimson with anger by the time they finished.

"So, my own officers couldn't track these thefts to a warehouse area, but two teenagers could," he said in a tight voice. "Maybe I should've hired *them.*" His dark eyes bored into Hawkins, then Powderly.

"All right. We'll check it out," Detective Hawkins grumbled. "But it sounds to me as if that guy led them on a wild-goose chase."

"I don't think so," Nancy said firmly.

"Come on, Hawk, lighten up," Stan Powderly said, clapping his partner on the shoulder. "These girls just might help us get somewhere."

With a deep sigh, Raul Quinones rubbed his temples. "Stan's right, B.D.," he said. "At this point we need to check out every lead."

"You're the boss," Hawkins said, folding his arms over his chest. Nancy could tell he wasn't convinced.

Detective Powderly turned to Nancy. "Sorry if we seem doubtful, but all we've come up with so far is dead ends. A dozen cars have been stolen in River Heights in the last month, and they've all disappeared without a trace."

"Well, if the chop shop is in one of those warehouses Nancy and I saw, this could be the tip you've been waiting for," Bess said brightly.

Hawkins glared at Bess. "I've got to finish the Jenkins report," he said gruffly. "Stan, you'll have to cruise past those warehouses, okay?"

"Cruise past?" Bess echoed, looking from Hawkins to Powderly in disbelief. "Aren't you going to charge into the warehouses and arrest the thieves?"

The younger detective shook his head. "We can't. You don't know positively that the car went into a warehouse. Besides, we'd need a search warrant even to look around," he explained. "I think you've been watching too much TV, Ms. Marvin."

"But what about my car?" Bess insisted.

"Detective Hawkins is right," Raul Quinones told Bess and Nancy. "We can't do anything unless you know for sure that the car the kid was driving was yours, which you don't, and exactly which warehouse he went into, which you don't."

Nancy put her hand on Bess's arm. "They're right," she said.

Planting her hands on her hips, Bess glared angrily at the three detectives and Nancy. "Well, since you aren't going to do anything about it, I will!" With that, she marched out the door.

Nancy started after Bess, but Detective Hawkins caught her arm. "Don't you two ladies go getting into trouble," he warned. Then he stepped around Nancy and went to his desk in the outer cubicle. Stan Powderly followed him.

"B.D.'s right, Ms. Drew," Raul Quinones added. "A teenage private eye used to purse snatchings and missing old ladies is no match for car thieves."

Nancy bristled. Purse snatchings! This guy had some nerve. "I'm not promising I won't help my friend, Detective, since we discovered more in one night than you did in the past month," she said hotly.

For a long moment Nancy and Raul Quinones silently faced each other.

"I realize we don't have solid proof that the car drove into one of the warehouses," she said at last. "Let's hope that Detective Powderly finds something out." Offering her hand, she added, "Nice meeting you, Detective."

"Likewise," he replied. As they shook, he fixed her with a penetrating gaze. "And, Ms. Drew," he added as she left, "don't do anything stupid."

When Nancy emerged from the police station, Bess was waiting in the Mustang, which was parked next to the curb out front. "We're going back to search those warehouses," Bess said determinedly.

"My idea exactly," Nancy agreed, climbing in the driver's seat.

"So don't argue with me," Bess continued, "or try to change my . . ." Her voice trailed off, and she stared at Nancy in surprise. "Really?"

Nancy nodded. "The police are right. They need probable cause before they can get a search warrant. If we're careful, maybe we can find the evidence they need."

"All right!" Bess exclaimed, grinning. "We can pretend we're inspectors or looking for work or—" She broke off with a gasp. "Oh, no! I totally forgot. I'm supposed to meet Dirk for lunch."

"*Ohhh.* Big decision," Nancy teased. "Will she choose the guy or the car?"

Bess furrowed her brow, then quickly snapped her fingers. "I've got it. I'll invite Dirk to come along. Then I can have both. Let me just run back into the station and call him."

While Nancy waited, she rolled down the window and breathed in deeply. It was a beautiful May morning, sunny, yet not hot. She checked her watch, then glanced out the window.

She hoped Bess wouldn't take long. On the other hand, she wanted to give Detective Powderly a chance to check out the warehouse area and leave before they got there. Even though he'd been friendly and helpful, Nancy didn't think he'd approve of their snooping around.

Nancy looked up as the front door to the police station opened, but the person coming out wasn't Bess. Nancy recognized B. D. Hawkins's tall, slim build and cowboy boots. He strode around to the employees' parking lot at the side of the station and got into a dark blue sedan. When he pulled out of the lot and drove past Nancy, she could see there was a dent in his right front fender.

He must have finished the Jenkins report early, Nancy thought. Maybe he was going to join Detective Powderly in the warehouse district.

The front doors to the police station opened again, and this time Bess did come running out. "Dirk said he'd love to come," she told Nancy. "In fact he said something about always wanting to nab a car thief."

"So, what's the plan?" Dirk asked from the back seat of Nancy's Mustang. "We climb up a fire escape to check in windows?"

Nancy and Bess had just picked him up at his family's house, and they were heading for the industrial area of town.

"Nothing quite that dramatic, I'm afraid," Nancy told Dirk, laughing.

"What *is* our plan?" Bess asked, looking expectantly at Nancy.

"Actually, I haven't thought of one," Nancy admitted. "First, let's just see what that dead-end street is like in daylight."

A few minutes later Bess pointed out her window. "There's the sign for Pacific Trucking Company," she said. "Take the next right, Nan."

Nancy turned into the dead-end street, then pulled over to the curb and turned off the ignition. She, Bess, and Dirk peered out the front windshield.

It was definitely the street they'd been down the night before, but now it was busy with trucks loading and unloading. The ramps were dotted with men and women stacking dollies with boxes, writing on clipboards, and talking.

"I've got an idea," Dirk said. "We can go in and inquire about shipping my race car to California."

"You're going to California?" Bess asked with dismay.

Dirk laughed. "No way. This is just to help out the investigation," he told Bess.

"It's a great idea, Dirk," Nancy said. She pointed to a building on the left, a two-story warehouse with double garage doors. The sign over the doors said Ace Hauling.

Grinning at Bess and Nancy, Dirk said, "Well, let's find out what they haul."

Nancy pulled the Mustang back into the street to park by the loading dock of Ace. As she did, a huge car carrier pulled away from another loading dock farther down the street. It filled most of the road.

"Can that thing get past us?" Bess asked nervously.

"I think so," Nancy replied, steering the Mustang as close to the right curb as she could.

The carrier accelerated and came clanking toward them. Nancy honked the horn to warn the huge vehicle away. Instead, it suddenly swerved over onto Nancy's side of the road. Nancy couldn't pull out of its path.

As the carrier continued to bear down on them, Bess grabbed for Nancy's arm. "That truck's headed straight for us!" she screamed. "We're going to get run over!"

Chapter Five

NANCY'S HEART leapt into her throat. The carrier was barreling toward them so fast, it would squash the Mustang flat as a pancake! Couldn't the driver see them? She glanced around frantically. Just ahead there was a ramp up to a building on the right, but Nancy didn't know if she could get there before the carrier blocked it.

"Hold on!" she yelled. She pushed the gas pedal to the floor, and the Mustang shot forward.

Bess screamed in the seat beside Nancy as the Mustang and the carrier flew toward each other. Just when a crash seemed inevitable, Nancy cranked the steering wheel as hard as she could to the right. The Mustang flew up over the curb and bounced onto a paved ledge that led up the ramp.

"Look out!" Dirk called, bracing himself.

Nancy stomped on the brakes, but not hard enough. The car zoomed up the ramp and plowed into a stack of boxes, scattering them everywhere before screeching to a halt.

Nancy whipped her head around in time to see the carrier rumble past. She caught a glimpse of the driver. He was leaning out the window watching them, a nasty grin on his craggy face. Obviously he had seen them. Black hair stuck out from beneath his baseball cap. Before Nancy could read the license plate number, the carrier had turned the corner and was out of sight.

"Are you guys all right?" she asked Bess and Dirk.

Surprise showed in Dirk's green eyes, but he quickly recovered his composure. "Sure," he replied. "Great driving, Nancy. Ever think about racing?"

Beside Nancy, Bess slowly let out the breath she must have been holding the whole time. "I'm okay, too. If I can get my heart to stop pounding like a drum, that is."

Nancy jumped as someone rapped on her windshield. A man's face was pressed close to the glass. He had scraggly blond hair and was unshaven.

As he bent down to reach her window, he asked, "Are you all right?" The man was over six feet tall and burly, with arm muscles that bulged out of his T-shirt sleeves. There was an unreadable expression in his eyes.

Nancy nodded. "Fine. I'm not so sure about my car, though. That was quite a jolt."

"Well, you better back it up and get it out of here. We've got work to finish up," the guy said gruffly. Then he stepped away.

Nancy didn't know if he was threatening her or simply being brusque, but she didn't want to find out. She was about to do as the man asked when Dirk leaned forward and called out her window, "Not until I check the car." In a lower voice, he added, "You don't want to drive off if something's wrong."

"We might not have any choice," Bess said nervously. Several other guys had appeared on the loading dock. "Let's get out of here, Nan."

"Dirk's right. It could be dangerous to drive," Nancy told Bess. Turning off the ignition, she got out of the car, Dirk right behind her.

"Sorry about the boxes," Nancy said to the men on the loading dock, gesturing toward the cardboard cubes that were scattered everywhere.

The blond man watched Nancy with steely gray eyes. "It's a good thing for you they were empty."

"You knocked your front end out of alignment," Dirk called from the right side of the car, where he was kneeling.

Going over to him, Nancy saw that the right

front tire was scuffed and the rim of the wheel was bent. "You can still drive it, but get it to your mechanic as soon as possible," Dirk said, straightening up.

"Thanks for checking," Nancy told him. The burly blond man was right behind them, his arms crossed over his chest. The other men were already restacking the cardboard boxes.

Nancy tried to ignore his intimidating stare. "Did you happen to notice that carrier's license plate number?" she asked him.

He shook his head. "Nope."

"Then how about the company that owns the carrier? Is the driver someone you know?" Nancy persisted.

"Don't know that, either." The blond man turned and began helping the others stack boxes. "But I know one thing," he tossed over his shoulder. "If I were you I'd get out of here. This isn't the kind of place young folks should be hanging around." As if to emphasize his words, he took a knife from his pocket, plunged it into one of the boxes, and ripped it in two.

Dirk took Nancy's elbow and firmly propelled her to the driver's side of the Mustang. "Uh, thanks again," Nancy called while Dirk climbed into the back seat. She then slid into the front.

"Hurry up," Bess whispered, nervously peering out the window at the men on the loading dock.

Nancy started the car, but looked at the

building in front of them carefully before pulling away. "There's no sign on this warehouse. I wonder who owns it. I hate leaving without finding out anything."

"Oh, we found out plenty," Bess said as Nancy backed down the ramp. "Like not to come here during the day."

"I'm pretty sure that that car carrier's trying to run us down was no accident," Nancy said, steering her Mustang onto the main road.

"What are you talking about?" Dirk asked.

Nancy looked at him in the rearview mirror. "That driver could have stopped. He had to have seen us. And those guys on the loading dock sure acted as if they were hiding something." She tapped the steering wheel. "Which proves there's a chop shop somewhere on this street. Maybe right where we crashed, or in the building where the carrier was parked."

"I don't know," Dirk said, shaking his head. "You'd think the thieves would have brains enough to play it cool. I mean, trying to run us over was like waving a sign that said, Chop Shop in Here."

Bess laughed. "You're right. Hey, are you guys hungry? I was so nervous back there, I must have burned off a zillion calories. Let's eat."

They stopped at a pizzeria downtown. Bess and Dirk kept up a steady stream of talk while they ate, but Nancy hardly spoke. She was glad Bess and Dirk were hitting it off, but something about their encounter at the warehouse was still bothering her.

Someone had to have warned the guy driving the carrier that they were coming. Only one person that she could think of knew that they were headed there, and that person was Dirk. After Bess called him, he could easily have phoned his contacts at the chop shop—if it *was* him. Nancy couldn't figure out why he would have stayed in the car, though.

"Hey. Can you guys drop me off at Harry's Garage?" Dirk asked as they left the pizzeria. "I need to pick up some parts. My brother works there, so he can give me a ride home."

"Sure," Nancy agreed. The garage was just a few blocks away. When they got there, Dirk climbed out on Bess's side. After he'd shut the door, he leaned his arms on her open window.

"Thanks for the wild ride, Nancy," he said, his green eyes twinkling. "I guess I'll see you girls tomorrow at the track?"

Bess grinned at him. "You got it."

As Nancy drove away, Bess turned to her with dreamy, glassy eyes. "Wow. What a guy," she said. "Aren't you glad we invited him?"

"Yeah. I like Dirk, too," Nancy agreed. Taking a deep breath, she added, "That's what makes this hard to bring up."

Bess straightened up in her seat and questioned Nancy, "What are you talking about?"

"Somebody tipped off that guy in the carrier that we were coming," Nancy said quietly.

"But who? Nobody knew except—" Bess's face blanched white. "No. No way," she protested. "Dirk in cahoots with car thieves?"

"It makes sense. He's an expert driver, and he knows cars. Guys who race cars always need parts."

Bess shook her head. "I still don't believe Dirk would work with criminals just to get parts. I mean, you don't have any proof."

"That is what we need," Nancy agreed. "Proof. We need to catch someone stealing a car and follow him to the right warehouse. Then the police will have everything they need to move in."

"Oh, right. As if some thief is going to let us hang around while he steals a car," Bess said, rolling her eyes.

Nancy grinned at Bess. "Actually, that's exactly what I have in mind," she said. "Only the thief won't know we're there."

At nine o'clock that night, Nancy picked Bess up at her house.

Before Bess got into the car, she gestured to her clothes. "What do you think, Nan? Black shirt, black pants, black socks and shoes—the height of fashion," she joked.

"It is if you're tracking down car thieves," said Nancy, laughing. She, too, was dressed all in black, and she wore a dark ski cap to cover her reddish blond hair.

"I thought Dirk said you shouldn't be driving your car," Bess said as Nancy headed the Mustang toward the riverfront area.

Nancy patted the dashboard. "It's going into the shop tomorrow. Alignment isn't a terrible problem, so we're safe for now. I'm not sure how we're going to get around after this, though."

"Don't worry about that," Bess said. "The insurance company's paying for a rental car that I can drive for thirty days—or until we recover the Camaro," she added confidently. "My dad picked it up after work tonight, but he had to go to a meeting so I haven't seen it yet. For once I'll get to chauffeur *you* around."

Ten minutes later the girls were driving down the winding road that went from the highway to the riverfront.

"What now?" Bess asked. "How do you know where the car thieves are going to hit?"

"We have to think like one," Nancy replied. "Officer Jackson said two cars were stolen from the main parking lot of the riverfront renovation. Then your Camaro was taken from the restaurant lot. The way I figure it, that leaves the lot at the nightclub, the Scene. I bet it's crowded on a Thursday night, too."

Bess nodded. "So we're going to stake out the Scene's parking lot?"

"Right." Nancy drove past the nightclub, which was perched next to the Riverside on a cliff overlooking the river. The parking lot was across the street from it.

"Officer Jackson was right when she said the lots here aren't well lit," Bess commented as Nancy pulled her car into the lot. There was only one streetlight at the entrance. Most of the cars were just black silhouettes in the darkness.

"Tonight that will be in our favor," Nancy reminded Bess.

Nancy found a spot next to a sedan in the middle of the lot. "If we hunch down between my car and the sedan, we should be able to see anyone coming or going. We'll leave the door propped open in case we need to make a quick getaway."

The overhead light winked on as Bess opened her door to get out. She giggled and reached up to remove the plastic cover and unscrew the bulb. "Better take this out. Nothing like advertising that we're here."

The two girls sat on the gravel next to the Mustang. Nancy kept a look out by the rear fender, which faced the back part of the lot and a dark side street. Bess's spot by the front tire gave her a good view of the entrance to the Scene.

For two hours they watched as laughing couples and groups parked their cars and went into the nightclub. Nancy was beginning to wonder if they were wasting their time when Bess said in a low voice, "Hey, look."

Nancy joined Bess at the front of the car in time to see a man and woman leaving the nightclub. The woman was laughing and holding on to the man's arm. When the woman passed under the single streetlight, Nancy recognized Kitty Lambert's long, brown hair.

"She sure seems to get around," Bess whispered.

"The guy looks familiar, too," Nancy whispered back.

"He looks like Dirk!" Bess said angrily.

"It's not him, though. He's too tall," Nancy cut in. "I bet it's Dirk's brother. Dirk said something about Kitty having a thing for his older brother, remember?"

"Here they come." Bess and Nancy huddled close to the Mustang as Kitty and her date turned down the row opposite the Mustang and stopped at a shiny new Firebird. A few minutes later the car pulled out.

A police car cruised past soon after that. "That's the second police car we've seen," Nancy mentioned. "They probably patrol every hour."

She moved back to the rear end of the car, so she could keep an eye on the rear of the lot. It was the darkest area. A thief could sneak into the lot, hot-wire a car, and drive it onto the side street and out of sight before anyone saw him.

"How much longer?" Bess whispered twenty minutes later. "My back has a cramp in it, and my right leg's asleep. I may never walk again."

"We can't give up now," Nancy said quietly. "Besides, if we don't stick it out tonight, we'll just have to do this again tomorrow night."

"Tomorrow!" Bess groaned. "I hope—"

"Shhh." Nancy held a finger to her lips. Was that the crunch of gravel she'd heard?

The two girls fell silent, but there was no sound. Then very faintly Nancy heard it again. *Crunch. Crunch.* Someone was creeping into the lot, very slowly, trying not to make a sound.

Nancy peered around the rear fender of the Mustang. Silhouetted against the night sky was a tall figure wearing a baseball cap and a long coat. It was much too warm to have on a coat.

Nancy put her finger to her lips and gestured for Bess to stay put. The figure was too tall and broad shouldered to be a woman, Nancy decided. She watched him stealthily make his way to a red sports car two rows down from the Mustang.

The person stopped at the driver's window of the sports car. After glancing around, he reached under his coat and pulled out a flat metal rod. It was a slim jim, a tool used to break the lock of a car, Nancy realized.

They'd found their thief! Now they just had to follow him and his stolen car to the right warehouse, call the police, and bingo! The auto theft ring would be out of commission.

Nancy silently gestured for Bess to slip into the car.

Nodding, Bess started to creep toward the open door. Suddenly she stumbled and pitched face first into the gravel. With a muffled cry, she threw her arms out to catch herself.

Nancy whirled her head around to check on the thief. She hoped he hadn't heard!

Her heart sank when she saw that the figure had paused and was turned in her direction now. He tucked the slim jim under his coat, then took off for the side street.

"Bess, call the police!" Nancy hissed over her shoulder as she started after the guy. Keeping low, she jogged down the aisle until she was even with him. She tried to get a look at him, but a row of cars was between them, and in the dark she couldn't make out his face.

Suddenly he began to run. He must have heard her! Sprinting, Nancy raced through the row of cars that separated them and grabbed at the flying tails of his coat. The person whipped around, and something metal fell to the gravel with a clang.

Before Nancy could get a better grip on him, blinding car lights from the side street flashed in her face.

"Police! Freeze!" commanded an amplified voice.

Nancy froze, but the thief took off. Nancy saw a red ponytail escape from under his baseball cap before he disappeared down the side street.

"Stop him! He tried to steal a car," Nancy yelled, pointing after the fleeing figure. Someone burst from the police cruiser and ran after the thief.

The next thing Nancy knew, someone had grabbed her arms, twisted them behind her, and snapped on handcuffs.

"Don't move," a deep voice growled. "You're under arrest for suspicion of car theft."

Chapter Six

NANCY WHIRLED AROUND to see B. D. Hawkins glaring at her. "Let me go. I'm not the thief," she protested.

"Sure," he scoffed. "You've got the right to remain—"

"What do you think you're doing?" Bess yelled angrily, hurrying across the parking lot toward Nancy and the detective. "That's my friend!"

When she got to Nancy, Bess reached over and whipped off Nancy's ski cap so that her friend's reddish blond hair tumbled to her shoulders.

"Remember me, Nancy Drew?" Nancy said.

The detective's mouth fell open in surprise. He quickly unlocked the cuffs as the squad car pulled up.

Raul Quinones got out, his face purple with rage. "What are you two doing here?" he demanded, glaring first at Bess and then at Nancy.

Before either of them could reply, Stan Powderly jogged into the lot from the side street. He was breathing hard. "I couldn't catch him," he said. "Heard a car drive off, though."

"Did you see the car?" Quinones asked.

Powderly shook his head.

"You let him get away?" Bess said in disbelief. "After all we went through!"

"After all *you* went through?" B. D. Hawkins sputtered. "We've been parked in that side street for an hour. We would have nailed the guy if you two hadn't butted in."

Nancy glared back at him. *"We've* been waiting around for *two* hours. We almost had him when you decided to jump me. So don't blame us."

"How was I suppose to know it was you? We usually don't share stakeouts with kids dressed like army commandos," Hawkins scoffed.

"Enough," Detective Quinones said sharply. "We all made mistakes, and because of it the real thief got away. Now we're back to square one."

"Not really," Nancy put in. "When I grabbed the guy's coat, something fell from it." Bending down, she hunted around in the gravel. "There," she said, pointing under a nearby car. "It's the slim jim. I could see the thief wasn't wearing gloves, so I bet you'll be able to lift prints from it."

Quinones pulled a handkerchief from his back pocket. After wrapping the fabric around the tip of the slim jim, he carefully picked it up. Nancy saw several greasy marks on the metal.

"Get an evidence bag, B.D.," Quinones instructed. He turned to Nancy and Bess. "I want you two in my office first thing in the morning for a complete report on what happened tonight."

"Shouldn't we go now?" Bess asked eagerly. "Maybe Nancy can find the guy in the mug books."

Raul wearily rubbed his eyes. "That'll take hours, and it's almost midnight already. Be there at eight-thirty tomorrow morning."

Nancy watched as Detective Hawkins carefully bagged the slim jim, then sealed it with evidence tape. When he noticed her watching, he stopped writing on the tape. "Good night," he said firmly.

As Nancy and Bess walked back to the Mustang, Bess said, "I'm really sorry about falling, Nan. My leg went to sleep, and when I tried to move, it just buckled under me."

"Don't worry about it," Nancy told her. "I'm hoping the police will get prints from the slim jim. If the guy has a record, the police should be able to nail him—and maybe find your car."

Bess smiled. "Let's hope so."

Friday morning Nancy was tapping her foot impatiently as she waited in front of the garage where she'd just dropped off her car. Bess was supposed to have picked her up already. It was twenty after eight, and the police expected them at the station at eight-thirty.

"Nancy!"

Nancy watched as Bess pulled up in an old silver convertible. "What do you think of these wheels?" Bess asked.

"Pretty nice," Nancy said, hopping in on the passenger side. "It had better get us to the police station fast."

"No problem." Bess shifted into first and stepped on the gas. The car jerked forward, then promptly stalled out.

Flashing Nancy a confident grin, Bess turned the key again. "Don't worry. I'm not used to driving a stick shift, but I'll get the hang of it. My dad gave me a few lessons this morning."

The car made a grinding noise, coughed, then sputtered to life. "See?" Bess checked behind her, then pulled into traffic. She shifted into second, and the car shuddered once before jerking ahead.

"Uh, Bess, why did you get a stick shift?"

Bess grinned. "I told my dad to rent the sportiest model he could find. You know, to take my mind off the Camaro. I didn't know the sportiest one would also be the oldest—and the hardest to drive. So far it's been fun, though."

Nancy couldn't help laughing. "Let's just hope we make it to the police station in one piece!"

By the time they arrived at the station, it was twenty to nine. The two girls hurried up to the auto theft office, where they found the three detectives in the outer cubicle. From the sober look on Detective Quinones's face, Nancy guessed that something was very wrong.

"Sorry we're late," she apologized.

"We had car trouble," Bess added, giggling.

Raul Quinones got right to business. "Let's start with the description of the guy you tried to take on last night," he said to Nancy. "Stan's got the mug books."

"First, could I explain why we were there?" Nancy asked. She briefly told them about the incident at the warehouse. "We think the car carrier went after us because we were getting close to the chop shop."

Quinones shot Stan Powderly a stern look. "I thought you said you didn't find anything when you checked out that area."

"I didn't," he said defensively. He pulled a notepad from his back pocket. "I made a sketch of the area and noted what business is in each building."

Nancy pointed out the building where they'd zoomed up the ramp. "R. H. Shipping," she said, reading the name Powderly had penciled in. "All of these shipping places sound as if they'd provide good cover. They could move cars or parts in and out, and no one would know."

Powderly gave her a dubious look. "I talked to someone at every place," he assured Detective Quinones. "They seemed legit to me."

"Check them out again," Quinones snapped at the two detectives. "We may be overlooking something. Now, about the guy we almost caught in the parking lot."

Nancy described the man. "I'm pretty sure he's the same guy we saw driving Bess's car. Even though it was dark both times, the red ponytail was pretty unique."

B. D. Hawkins listened with a bored expression on his face. It was obvious to Nancy that he didn't think much of her opinions. "The lab should have some prints for us by now," he said when she was finished. "I'll go ask."

He left, and Detective Quinones retreated to his cubicle. For the next two hours Nancy and Bess paged through the mug books with Stan. Nancy didn't see a single picture of the guy with the red ponytail.

Several times Detective Quinones stalked in and out of the office. When they were done, Nancy and Bess went over to his cubicle. He was staring at the computer screen on his desk, a scowl on his face.

"Sorry, but the guy I saw last night isn't in

the mug books," Nancy told him, poking her head in.

He stared at Nancy for a moment, as if gauging something. Then he stood up and said, "That's okay. Uh, come on in a second. I want to tell Bess her VIN." He gestured for the two girls to enter his office, then said to Stan, "Why don't you return those mug books."

"What's a VIN?" Bess asked Detective Quinones when he turned back to the girls.

"Your Vehicle Identification Number," Quinones answered, distracted. "All cars have it etched on the dashboard, the door, and the engine block. It's on your registration and in the computer. That's how we can identify a stolen car—or what's left of it."

As he spoke, Quinones again stepped into the other cubicle. Sticking his head into the hall, he glanced back and forth. What was going on? Nancy wondered. He was acting like a caged animal.

When he came back he brought two chairs from the outer cubicle and gestured for Nancy and Bess to sit down. Nancy hoped this wasn't going to be bad news about Bess's car.

Detective Quinones sat down at his desk. Without meeting the girls' eyes, he cleared his throat and began to speak.

"As you know, our investigation into the recent auto thefts hasn't been going well—at least not as well as I'd like." Reaching over, he swiped at a cobweb clinging to his rubber plant. "Well, this morning I had a long meeting with Chief McGinnis, and we discussed several things."

Finally Quinones looked up at Nancy. "He said you were a friend of his, Nancy. He also said you were a crackerjack detective, and that I should enlist your help in tracking down the car thieves."

Nancy could tell that Quinones wasn't happy with the chief's suggestion. "I'm not sure I understand," she said. "Last night I was only trying to help Bess get *her* car back. We didn't mean to get involved in your investigation."

"I know," Quinones said with a nod. "But now there are—complications."

"Like what?" Bess asked, puzzled.

"First thing this morning I checked with the lab," said Quinones. "They told me that no fingerprints were found on the slim jim."

Nancy sat up straight. "But that's impossible!" she exclaimed. "You saw those greasy marks on it yourself. There *had* to be prints."

Detective Quinones was very sober. "The labs boys tell me that somebody wiped the slim jim clean."

"But who would do that?" Bess asked, her blue eyes opening wide. "And why?"

Nancy's mind was racing. "The same person who could tip off the thieves about when the cops would be patrolling the riverfront area," she said.

"Nobody knows about the patrols except the cops, right?" said Bess, confused.

Nancy nodded. If what she was thinking was correct, this was very serious.

"Someone's sabotaging your investigation in order to help the thieves, right?" Nancy guessed.

Detective Quinones's face told Nancy that she was correct.

"Since the saboteur was able to wipe the slim jim clean," she went on, "that means there's a bad cop in the police department."

Chapter Seven

DETECTIVE QUINONES nervously ran his fingers through his dark hair.

"None of us likes to believe there's a bad cop on the force," he said, looking at Nancy and Bess, "but several other things have happened to make me suspicious. The slim jim only confirmed it."

Quinones cleared his throat and added, "I hope you'll be able to help me out, Nancy. Of course, if you run into Stan or B.D. your explanation will be that you're only helping Bess get her car back."

Bess's blue eyes opened wide. "You don't suspect that it's one of them?"

"B.D. handled the evidence bag last, but it could be anyone," the detective said wearily.

"I've been taking precautions to stop whoever it is. I even changed last night's stakeout plans at the last minute. Every time we've had a surveillance before, the thieves have hit somewhere totally different. That made me suspect a leak."

Nancy leaned forward excitedly. "There's something else, too. Stan and B.D. both heard us say we were going to the warehouse yesterday," she said. "They could have warned the people there."

"Then it isn't Dirk," Bess said, brightening.

Quinones raised his brows. "Dirk?"

"Oops!" Bess's hand flew to her mouth.

Nancy explained who Dirk was and why they thought he might have warned the people at the chop shop.

"He might be in on the ring," Quinones said. "We've had our eye on the racetrack. Some parts from stolen cars have shown up there, though we haven't been able to trace them to anyone."

He reached for a pencil and pad. "Let me get some information on this Dirk fellow."

"If he's innocent, nothing will happen," Nancy reassured Bess.

"If he's guilty, we need to catch him," Detective Quinones stated. "As for the bad cop, you leave that problem to me."

Bess and Nancy told the detective all they knew about Dirk. "We're going to the drag strip this afternoon," Nancy finished.

Quinones nodded. "Good place for you to start your investigation. Be sure you call me at the *slightest* sign that something's not right. Here's my card. I'll write my home number on the back."

Nancy saw his face harden as he noticed something behind her. "Hawkins!" Detective Quinones snapped. "Did the lab find anything about the fingerprints?"

Nancy and Bess whipped around to see the younger detective entering the outer office. B.D. shook his head. "Nope. Said they're understaffed today and it'll take a while. Typical."

Quinones must have arranged with the lab to keep the results a secret, Nancy realized.

"The girls were just giving me a detailed description of the thief," Quinones said. With a significant look at Nancy and Bess, he added, "Now they're leaving."

Quickly Nancy and Bess stood up, said goodbye, and left the office. When they got outside, Bess turned to Nancy. "I feel like I've been plunked down in the middle of some police movie."

"I know what you mean," Nancy agreed. "I wanted to ask some more questions, but there wasn't time."

"Speaking of time," said Bess, "Dirk told us to meet him at the track at two o'clock."

Nancy checked her watch. "It's only eleven-thirty."

"Right," Bess said. "That gives me less than three hours to shower, pick out an outfit, fix my hair—"

Nancy laughed. "You must *really* want to knock Dirk's socks off."

"You've got that right," Bess said. "I like the guy. No matter *what* you think, I know he's not involved in all this. He's just too nice to do something so rotten."

"Well, you still need to be careful," Nancy warned. "I don't want my best friend getting involved with a car thief."

"This is the racetrack?" Bess asked that afternoon as she drove the silver convertible down a dirt road into a field crowded with cars. The top was down, and dust billowed around the girls.

Glancing around, Nancy said, "I think it's called a drag strip."

"So what's the difference?" Bess asked, checking herself in the rearview mirror. "Oh no! Look at my hair. It's a rat's nest." She parked the car, then took a brush out of her purse and began brushing out the tangles in her blond hair.

Nancy was glad she'd decided to put her hair back in a French braid. Peeking into the side mirror, she brushed back a few wayward strands.

"Oh no. Here comes Dirk, and my hair's still a wreck," Bess moaned.

Nancy turned and saw Dirk striding across the grass toward them. He was wearing faded jeans, a light blue T-shirt, and a baseball cap. A tall guy was walking next to him, and Nancy recognized him as Kitty Lambert's date from the night of the stakeout. He was a little heavier than Dirk, but they both had the same sun-streaked hair and green eyes.

"You look great." Nancy quickly reassured Bess as they got out of the car.

Bess smoothed out the pale yellow stretch pants and oversize yellow- and white-striped T-shirt she was wearing. "You think so?"

"Hey, you made it," Dirk said, giving Bess a hug.

"I wouldn't miss it for anything," Bess said.

The other guy stepped over to Nancy. "Hi. I'm Jake Walters, Dirk's older, bigger, and smarter brother," he said. Taking her hand, he gave it a warm squeeze.

"I'm Nancy," she said.

"And I'm Bess."

"Glad to meet you, Nancy and Bess," Jake said, flashing Nancy a brilliant smile.

What a flirt, Nancy thought. It made her wonder how serious Jake and Kitty Lambert were.

Around them, people were leaning over the chain-link fence or sitting on the nearby grass. A small concession stand stood opposite the starting line. Some buildings that were probably maintenance sheds or garages dotted the surrounding area. The entire perimeter was bordered by cornfields.

Nancy glanced idly around. The track was informal and crowded. It would probably be easy for anyone to come in and sell hot auto parts without attracting attention.

"So where's the oval track?" Bess asked curiously as the four of them started across the parking lot.

"There isn't one. There's only a straight, quarter-mile track," Dirk explained. He pointed to a short stretch of road lined with a chain-link fence. "In drag racing, two cars speed down a straight track as fast as they can. The car with the fastest time wins."

Bess paused, confusion on her face. "I thought there'd be—"

A deafening roar drowned out her words. Nancy clapped her hands to her ears as two cars tore down the track, their rear ends jacked up and their huge back tires spinning. When they reached the finish line, parachutes burst from the back to slow them.

"Those are Funny Cars," Dirk explained when the noise died down. "Race cars that have been radically modified. Those babies can go over two hundred miles an hour."

"If you ask me, they should be called Noisy Cars," Bess said, laughing. "Is that what you race?"

Dirk shook his head. "Nope. I race stock cars. They're regular cars that are finely tuned for the best performance possible. They're still pretty noisy, though."

They passed the concession stand, then crossed the end of the track, where two more Funny Cars were being checked over for the next race. Just beyond was a fenced-off field crowded with trucks, cars, vans, trailers, and people.

"That's the pit area," Jake explained. A man in greasy overalls stood at the entrance to the field. Seeing Dirk and Jake, he waved the foursome in.

The brothers led Nancy and Bess to a neon green Firebird. Big D's Dynomite was written across the side in bright orange scroll letters.

"This is it," Dirk announced proudly.

Bess patted the hood. "She's a beauty!"

"Little brother had his test drive a while ago," Jake spoke up. "The Big D ran great. He should kill the competition."

Dirk shrugged, but his excited smile told Nancy that he felt pretty confident, too. "My race isn't until the end of the day, so we'll have some time together."

"Great," Bess said. "You can teach us all about drag racing." Her yellow pants were already smudged with dirt, but she didn't seem to mind.

"Any news on the Camaro?" Dirk asked Bess.

He seemed genuinely concerned, but Nancy shot Bess a cautioning glance. They had agreed not to tell Dirk that they were officially involved in the case.

"There's not much news," Bess said. "But the police did almost catch the guy I told you about—the one we're pretty sure stole my car. The one with long red hair in a ponytail."

Dirk suddenly frowned. "A red ponytail?" he repeated. "Why didn't you tell me? Are you sure?" Nancy had the feeling Bess's description rang a bell with Dirk.

Suddenly a loud clank caught Nancy's attention. She peered around the far side of Dirk's car. Jeans-clad legs were sticking out from underneath. Just as Nancy bent down to see who it was, a woman pulled herself from under the car.

It took Nancy a second to recognize Kitty Lambert. Kitty's long brown hair was tucked under a cap, and she wasn't wearing any makeup.

"Hi," Nancy said. "You probably don't remember me. I'm Dirk's friend, Nancy Drew. We met at the Riverside the other night."

"Oh, right. Hi," Kitty said distractedly. She pulled a metal tool tray from under the car. "Dirk, your torque wrench isn't working. I'll go get mine." She brushed off her jeans and walked away.

"Kitty, wait up," Jake called out, jogging after the brunette.

"Listen," Dirk said abruptly, "I have to get a part for the Big D. Why don't you two watch the Funny Cars race? There's a good view from that grassy hilltop. It overlooks the finish line. I'll meet you there in a couple of minutes."

"Great," Bess said as Dirk waved distractedly and walked off.

As Nancy and Bess headed for the hilltop Dirk had indicated, they passed several groups that had spread out blankets and set up lawn chairs.

"These yellow pants are going to be covered with grass and oil stains by the end of the day," Bess said with a resigned sigh as they found a spot on the hill. "But it's worth it. So what do you think about Jake?"

"He's nice, but I'm not sure I understand him," Nancy answered. "First he turned on the charm with me, and then he ran after Kitty." Shaking her head, she added, "I guess he's just an incurable flirt."

She stopped talking while two more cars roared down the track. As they waited for the next run, Nancy looked down into the pit area. From their perch on top of the hill, she and Bess could see everything. Nancy's gaze traveled over to the concession stand, where Kitty and Jake were standing. Kitty picked up something from the booth, then with a wave to Jake, left.

Nancy watched idly as Kitty made her way through the cars toward a man who was working on a motorcycle. When the man stood up, Nancy's eyes widened. He was huge! Kitty talked to him a second, then strode down a hill to a large, crudely built, garagelike structure.

"There's Dirk." Bess nudged Nancy, then pointed to a pickup truck in the parking lot. The truck had a cap enclosing the entire truck bed. "He's even cute from far away."

Dirk was talking to someone he was standing in front of and blocking. Nancy watched as Dirk pulled his wallet out of his pocket. The other person's hands shot out to open up the rear door in the cap and then reached in.

Nancy gasped when Dirk stepped back, revealing the other man. "Bess, look at that guy next to Dirk. He's got a red ponytail!"

Chapter Eight

NANCY JUMPED to her feet. "He could be the same guy who stole your car," she said excitedly.

"He's here at the racetrack?" Bess asked, following Nancy's gaze.

"I think so," Nancy told her. She started down the hill toward the truck. "I'm going to check it out."

Bess scrambled to her feet, but Nancy stopped her. "You'd better wait here. We don't want to make him suspicious."

Nancy jogged quickly down the hill to where Dirk and the guy with the red ponytail were standing. When she reached Dirk's side, she smiled cheerfully.

"Hi! I need to use a phone. Do you know where I can find one?" she asked. She glanced casually at the guy with the red hair, but his back was to her as he hunted for something in his pickup.

Dirk's eyes darted nervously around. "Uh, yeah," he replied. "It's next to the concession stand."

Just then the guy with the ponytail straightened up. "I've got just what you need," he said. Turning around, he handed Dirk a small plastic envelope.

When his eyes met Nancy's, a tiny flicker of fear crossed his face. Nancy knew she had him. She'd found the car thief! She had to call Detective Quinones and tell him right away.

"Uh, thanks," Nancy told Dirk. "I'd better hurry—I don't want to miss another Funny Car race."

With that, she darted off for the pay phone. A girl was already using the phone, so Nancy paced alongside the concession stand while she waited.

The face, the ponytail, the red hair . . . It was definitely the same guy she and Bess had seen twice before. Besides, it seemed obvious that he was selling car parts, and she was willing to bet that at least some of those parts were stolen.

Nancy stopped pacing for a moment as another thought occurred to her. If the parts were stolen, did Dirk know? Did he know the guy with the ponytail was a car thief?

Thinking back, Nancy remembered that Dirk had acted a little uncomfortable when

Bess mentioned the guy with a red ponytail. Just now, he'd acted nervous, too. Maybe Dirk was working with him. Maybe he was warning him about Nancy.

Hurry up, Nancy silently urged the girl in the phone booth. After she called Detective Quinones, she wanted to get a peek at the parts in the back of the pickup. It was really a long shot, she knew, but maybe she'd recognize something from Bess's car. Then she'd have better evidence the parts were stolen.

Finally the girl hung up, and Nancy darted in and grabbed the phone. She left a message for Detective Quinones with the dispatcher, then hung up and took a deep breath. She had to keep cool.

The guy with the ponytail obviously recognized her, but if he thought *she* hadn't recognized *him,* maybe he wouldn't panic and bolt.

Nancy glanced back at the parking lot. She could just make out the guy with the ponytail locking the door of his truck cap. After looking around, he headed for the garagelike building Kitty Lambert had disappeared into.

Nancy walked casually in the direction of the building, keeping a close watch on the guy. He opened the side door and disappeared inside the building.

What was he doing in there? Nancy wondered. She hurried down a low dirt slope to the back of the building and crouched beneath a small, boarded-up window.

"You didn't tell me someone almost caught

you!" a woman's shrill voice said from inside the building.

A guy murmured something. Then Nancy heard the woman's voice again, only this time, the roar of an engine drowned out her words.

Nancy inched slowly along the wall to the side, where it sounded as if the voices were coming from. Then she peered around the corner. Suddenly the side door was flung open and Kitty Lambert ran out, a wrench clasped in her hand.

So the woman with the shrill voice was Kitty! She must have been talking to the red-haired guy. Nancy watched as Kitty strode back to the pit area and Dirk's car. Nancy didn't see Dirk, though.

Turning her attention back to the building, she listened for the red-haired guy. There was no sound from inside the building. Nancy knew he had to be in there because she would have seen him if he'd come out the only door that she'd noticed.

Perfect, Nancy thought, smiling to herself. As long as he's in there, I might as well sneak a peek into the back of his truck.

Stepping away from the garage, Nancy checked to see where Dirk and Kitty were. Kitty was standing by Big D's Dynomite, talking to Jake. Nancy then spotted Dirk sitting with Bess on top of the hill. Good, the coast was clear.

Nancy walked casually toward the truck with the enclosed bed. There were plenty of other people milling around the parking lot, but they all seemed to be busy.

When Nancy reached the truck, she sauntered along the side and peeked into the window in the cap. The glass was tinted, but she could make out a pile of car parts inside.

Nancy glanced around quickly, then slipped her lock pick out of her purse. In five seconds she had the door to the truck bed open. She pressed her lips together as she surveyed the jumble of parts. How was she going to tell if they were stolen?

Her gaze fell on a rectangular engine block. Hadn't Detective Quinones mentioned that that was one of the places that the Vehicle Identification Number was stamped?

After checking to make sure no one was looking, Nancy stepped up on the bumper and leaned into the truck bed. Pulling her penlight from her purse, she clicked it on and searched for the VIN. All she found was a rough spot on one end. Maybe the number had been ground out.

Not definite proof, Nancy said to herself as she locked the truck back up. It was obvious that the guy with the ponytail, or someone he was working with, didn't want that part traced.

She walked casually away from the truck and checked her watch. Almost four-thirty. Where was Quinones? And where was the guy with the ponytail?

Dirk and Bess were still on the hill. Catching

Nancy's eye, Bess waved and made a drinking motion with her hand. Nancy nodded, then made her way toward the concession stand to buy some sodas.

As she passed by the garagelike shed, Nancy decided to make a little detour. She hoped the guy with the red ponytail was still inside. Nancy decided to keep an eye on him until the police arrived.

She slowly opened the door she'd seen Kitty storm out of. It was dark inside, and Nancy had to wait for her eyes to adjust.

Several large shapes turned out to be cars and tractors. Along the far wall were some gardening tools. This had to be some kind of maintenance shed. Nancy saw no sign of anyone inside, though.

She turned her attention to the cars. The one closest to her was a black sports car. An older model Chevy was parked next to the far wall. Between the two was a car covered with a tarp.

Could it be stolen? Maybe she could get a peek at the car's VIN. Silently, Nancy crept around the sports car to the middle one. The tarp was tied to the back bumper so she couldn't lift it up. As she passed between the two cars, heading to the front end, Nancy reached inside her purse for her penlight. If she could just see under—

Suddenly she lurched forward as the toe of her sneaker caught on something. With a cry, she landed on the dirt floor, her purse flattened beneath her.

Nancy rolled onto her side with a groan and sat up. She gasped when she saw what she'd stumbled over—two legs sticking out from under the middle car, as if someone were working on it.

A chill raced up her spine. No one would work on a car in darkness. Her fingers curled around her flashlight. Slowly she drew it from her purse and flicked it on.

Taking a shaky breath, she scrambled to her knees. She ran the beam of light up the jean-covered legs, then bent down and flashed it under the car.

It was the guy with the red ponytail.

A feeling of dread grew in the pit of Nancy's stomach. She felt for his pulse, but there was none. He was dead.

Chapter Nine

NANCY STARED at the dead man, her mind reeling.

Somebody had killed him and shoved him under the car. Kitty Lambert had come storming out with a wrench. Had it been Kitty?

Just then Nancy heard footsteps behind her. Before she could move, strong fingers closed around her shoulder. Instinctively, she whirled sideways and batted the person's arm away.

"Ow!" a male voice cried out.

Jumping up, Nancy found herself face-to-face with Raul Quinones. He was holding his arm and grimacing with pain.

"Detective Quinones! What are you doing sneaking up on me? I thought you were the person who killed the guy with the red ponytail."

The detective's mouth fell open. "Killed him?" he echoed.

He quickly knelt next to the body, and Nancy handed him her flashlight. When he aimed the beam under the car, he gave a low whistle. The light illuminated a small pool of blood under the head.

"Did you touch anything?" Quinones asked Nancy.

"I felt for a pulse," she replied. "Oh, and I tripped over his leg. That's how I found him."

Quinones sighed and got to his feet. "Well, there goes our car thief—and any chance of getting him to tell us where the chop shop is."

"Do you think he was just one of the little guys?" Nancy asked.

"I'm sure of it," the detective replied. "He might have led us to the ringleaders."

"I think I know who may have killed him," Nancy said. She told him about overhearing the conversation from outside the shed. "The woman said, 'You didn't tell me someone almost caught you.' Then I saw Kitty Lambert leave, carrying a large wrench. She's a mechanic who works with Dirk Walters, the guy we told you about."

"A blow on the back of the head with a wrench could have done it," Quinones said thoughtfully. He shone the penlight on the shed's dirt floor, and Nancy spotted two trails leading up to the car from the side of the shed by the tractor.

"Looks like she dragged him over here and

pushed him under the car," Nancy said. "Probably to hide him from anyone coming in the door."

Nancy started to follow the drag marks, but Detective Quinones put a restraining hand on her arm. "We'll take it from here," he said firmly. "I'll radio headquarters and get the boys from homicide and the crime lab out here."

"I'm sure glad you got here when you did," Nancy added. "You obviously got my message. I called because I witnessed Dirk buying a car part from this guy. I'm pretty sure the guy with the ponytail recognized me, too."

"We'll just have to ask Dirk a few questions," Quinones said as they walked to the door. "Just remember, let *me* do the talking. You're not supposed to be in on this case."

"How'd you know where to find me?" Nancy asked when they got outside.

"Your friend, Bess." He pointed over to his police car, where Nancy could see Dirk leaning against the rear bumper. Bess was hopping nervously from one foot to the other. When she saw Nancy, she rushed forward and gave her a hug.

"Is everything okay? You were going to get sodas, and then I saw you go into that building. When Detective Quinones drove up in a rush and asked where you were, I didn't know what to think."

"I'm fine," Nancy assured her, "but our car thief isn't."

"What do you mean?" Bess asked. "He's hurt?"

Nancy shook her head. "No. He's dead."

"Dead!" Dirk jumped up, and his face turned white. "But I just . . ." His voice trailed off, and he ran his fingers back through his hair.

Nancy was about to press Dirk for more information when Detective Quinones came over to them. "Now tell me what you know about this red-haired thief," the detective said, fixing Dirk with his eyes.

Dirk slumped back against the police car. "His name is Jimmy Sandia. He races here, that's all. I don't know him very well."

"Didn't you buy a car part from him?" Nancy pressed.

Dirk cracked a knuckle before answering. "Yeah. Jets for my carburetor. So what? Lots of people sell parts."

Nancy had a feeling Dirk wasn't telling everything he knew. He'd heard Bess say the car thief had a red ponytail. He must have guessed it was Jimmy.

Turning back to Detective Quinones, Nancy said, "I looked inside Sandia's truck and saw an engine block with the VIN ground out." She was taking a chance in letting Dirk overhear her, but she wanted to see how he'd react.

"Maybe he made a little money on the side selling the parts the chop shop couldn't use," Quinones guessed.

"Jimmy selling stolen parts?" Dirk broke

into the conversation. "That's crazy. I really resent that you'd think I'd buy hot parts. What kind of person do you think I am?"

Flashing Nancy an accusing look, he went on, "Anyway, Jimmy always locks his truck, so it sounds to me like you broke into it. Are you a cop or something? I mean, what's going on here?"

Nancy stared at Dirk without replying. He seemed more angry than worried, and he was surprised to hear about Jimmy selling stolen parts. Her gut feeling was that he was telling the truth—unless he was a very good actor.

Just then, two cars pulled up and half a dozen officers got out—the homicide squad and lab technicians, Nancy assumed. As they went about their jobs, she couldn't help but wonder if one of them was the bad cop, and if so which one. She had to trust that Detective Quinones could control that side of the investigation.

By this time other people were milling around them curiously. The police quickly roped the area off. Nancy turned as another car roared up, spraying dust everywhere. Stan Powderly opened the door and got out.

"Where's B.D.?" Quinones asked, a note of exasperation in his voice. "I couldn't get him on his radio."

Detective Powderly shrugged. "Who knows? He's been disappearing a lot lately. So what've we got?" He glanced at Nancy and Bess.

"The famous *detective,* Ms. Drew, still insists on snooping around," Quinones said, adopting a sudden, gruff attitude toward Nancy. "Well, she stumbled over something she didn't expect to find. Our car thief is dead."

Quinones gestured to the garage, and he and Powderly went in.

"You're a detective?" Dirk asked Nancy when the police officers had gone.

"The best," Bess said proudly.

Dirk's face flushed red with anger. "Now I get it. You guys are just hanging around the track trying to catch a car thief. You don't even care about being with me."

"No!" Bess exclaimed. "You invited us before my car was even stolen."

Dirk glanced doubtfully from Nancy to Bess, a frown creasing his forehead.

"But it does look as though some of your friends are involved," Nancy said softly.

"Jimmy Sandia was *not* my friend!" Dirk burst out.

"I'm not talking about Jimmy. I'm talking about Kitty," Nancy told him.

"Kitty?" Bess and Dirk said at the same time.

Nancy nodded. "I heard her talking to Jimmy in the garage before he was murdered. When she stormed out, she was carrying a wrench in her hand. She might have been the last person with him."

Dirk glared at Nancy. "Kitty Lambert would never hurt anyone," he said angrily. "I don't care what you saw. Now I'd appreciate it if you two would leave the track. I don't like you accusing my friends."

"What about your race?" Bess asked. "I thought you wanted us to see it."

"Forget it. Fans like you I can do without!" Turning abruptly, Dirk stormed off.

"I wish I could be sure about how involved he is in this whole thing," Nancy commented in a low voice, watching him go.

"Oh, come on, Nan," Bess scoffed. "So what if he bought a part from Jimmy Sandia. He probably didn't know it was from a stolen car."

Nancy wasn't convinced of that. She turned as Quinones and Powderly stepped out of the garage. At the same time, Detective Hawkins's blue sedan drove up.

"Where were you?" Quinones asked as the younger man got out of the car. "Why didn't you answer the dispatcher's call?"

Hawkins's face turned red. "I stopped for dinner, all right?" he said. "I mean, aren't we allowed to eat anymore?"

"Not when there's a murder," Powderly put in.

"A murder? Who?" Hawkins asked.

"Jimmy Sandia," Quinones told him. "The kid we *almost* caught at the nightclub."

"Any suspects?" Hawkins wanted to know.

Detective Quinones pointed to Nancy. "Ms. Drew saw a woman leave with a wrench. We'll know more after the crime technicians get through."

He dismissed Nancy and Bess with a terse "Thank you."

"What now?" Bess asked Nancy as the two girls slowly wandered away. "We're obviously not wanted here. I don't think Dirk cares if he ever sees our faces again." She shook her head. "I feel awful."

Nancy touched Bess on the arm. "Don't give up on him. He may be completely innocent," she said.

"At least you can't accuse him of murder. He was with me the whole time," Bess added.

Nancy nodded. "That's true. I do think he knows more than he's telling, though." She moved to the outskirts of the crowd to a spot where she could watch Dirk. He was leaning over the motor of his car. Just then, Jake and Kitty strode up to him.

"I think we should eat," Bess said from behind Nancy. "It's six-thirty and my stomach's reading empty."

"Mmm," Nancy said distractedly. She wasn't really listening. Her attention was focused on the group by Dirk's car. She kept thinking about Jimmy Sandia's murder. Kitty Lambert was an obvious suspect, but what would her motive be? Why would she kill a car thief? Was she in on the ring?

"Why do you keep spying on Dirk?" Bess asked indignantly, breaking into Nancy's thoughts.

"I think he may have tipped Jimmy Sandia off that I recognized him," Nancy replied.

"Now I bet he's warning Kitty." Sprinting forward, she started toward the group.

"Where are you going?" Bess called after her.

"To see what Dirk and Jake are up to," Nancy said over her shoulder. "I know you think Dirk's innocent, but someone killed Jimmy Sandia, and I'm going to find out who."

"I'm coming, too," Bess insisted.

Without waiting, Nancy hurried over to the pit area and wove through the many cars, trying to think of a plan of action. She was still about fifty yards away from the group, when Dirk caught sight of her. Frowning, he gestured toward her with an accusing finger. Kitty whirled around to focus right on Nancy. As Nancy got closer, she could see that the brunette's eyes were wide with fear. Before Nancy could even call her name, Kitty had taken off at a run.

Chapter Ten

NANCY RACED after Kitty, who had sped ahead. With a quick backward glance at Nancy, she whipped around a van and out of sight.

Her heart pounding, Nancy sprinted the distance to the van—then stopped abruptly. Kitty was nowhere to be seen. Nancy spun her head in every direction, but it was useless. Kitty had disappeared in the maze of cars.

Nancy walked back to Dirk's Big D. Dirk started to brush right past her when he saw her coming.

"Dirk, wait." Nancy caught his arm. "You need to help me out. If you're innocent, I need you to prove it to me."

Dirk shrugged off her arm. "Why bother," he scoffed. "You've already convicted us in your mind."

"That's not true," Nancy protested. "Kitty's only wanted for questioning. If she doesn't have anything to hide, she should go to the police."

Dirk stared down at her with probing green eyes. Jake stood behind him, his arms crossed against his chest.

"Hey!" Bess ran up, puffing and holding her side. "You guys are hard to keep up with." Seeing the sober expressions on everyone's faces, she asked, "Where did Kitty go? What's going on?"

Nancy kept her eyes on the Walters brothers. "I was just about to tell Dirk and Jake that they could be arrested for obstructing justice," she said firmly.

Finally Dirk let out a long breath. "Kitty's too scared to talk to the police," he said.

"Scared of what?" Bess asked.

"You don't have to say anything," Jake cut in angrily.

"What's she scared of, Dirk?" Nancy pressed, ignoring Jake's angry glare.

Dirk shrugged. "She wouldn't say."

"Then tell me where she is. If she runs, it will only be worse for her—and you."

"No way!" Jake said. He grabbed Dirk's arm and started to walk away, but Dirk shook him off.

"Look, maybe Nancy can help Kitty," he told Jake. Turning back to Nancy, Dirk said, "I'll try to find her. Be here tomorrow morning, and I'll see if I can get her to talk to you."

He smiled ruefully and added, "Besides, with Kitty on the run, I may need you guys to crew for me in tomorrow's race."

Dirk turned to Bess. For a second he just stared at her with a sad smile, then he bent down, kissed her lightly on the lips, and strode off with his brother. It was time for him to race.

For once Bess was speechless. "Whoa," she finally managed to say. "That was not the kiss of a car thief."

Nancy laughed. "Bess, you are a complete romantic."

"True," Bess agreed, grinning.

On Saturday morning Nancy called the police station before she had even had breakfast.

"Jimmy Sandia, alias Johnny Smithson, alias Jeremy Saunders, has quite a record for auto theft," Raul Quinones told her. "Amazing, considering he was only nineteen.

"Seems he's wanted in Chicago, where they're also looking for his female partner. She was described as an attractive woman in her midtwenties with bleached blond hair."

"Kitty Lambert?" Nancy suggested.

"Could be," Quinones said. "She could have dyed her hair brown. Unfortunately, there aren't any prints on her. It seems she's a little more cautious than Jimmy and has never been arrested."

"If she was his partner, that might give her a

motive for killing him," Nancy said. "She might have worried that he'd implicate her."

"I'll say. Jimmy was about to get nailed. She was probably afraid he'd tell us who he was working with in order to get a lighter sentence."

"What about the murder weapon?" Nancy asked.

She heard a brief shuffle of papers before Quinones answered. "Autopsy shows it was a heavy, metal tool—could've been a wrench. He was hit from behind when he was standing on the far side of the shed by the tractor. The murderer was probably hiding there, then dragged him over to hide the body."

Nancy looped the phone cord around her fingers as she thought. "Mmm. Any problem with ruined evidence this time?"

"No. That's strange, too," Quinones told her. "Our inside man let the investigation go through without a hitch. It's almost as if he wants the murderer to be caught."

"Or at least he wants *a* murderer caught," Nancy added. She told the detective about Dirk's belief that Kitty wouldn't hurt anyone, but that she was too scared to turn herself in for questioning.

"She should be scared," Quinones said. "She's our prime suspect. Hawkins and Powderly are tracking her down right now. I'm counting on you, too," he added in a serious voice. "Try to convince Dirk to lead you to Kitty."

"Bess and I are going to spend the day with him at the track," Nancy said. "Maybe he'll trust us enough to let us know what's going on."

"Good. Call me the second you have any news."

"Hi, Bess," Nancy said brightly as she climbed into the silver rental convertible a little later. "I guess you're feeling pretty optimistic about the weather, if you're leaving the top down."

Bess glanced up at the sky. Dark clouds had already hidden the sun. Two neon yellow rain slickers were draped across the back seat of the car. "Actually, I couldn't get the top up."

Nancy laughed as Bess backed the rental car from the Drews' driveway. This time the car lurched only once before Bess smoothly shifted into first.

They'd driven for about five minutes before the first raindrop splashed on Nancy's nose.

"Pull over, Bess. Let's see if we can get this top up," Nancy said. When the car stopped, she scrambled into the back seat and began to unsnap the top.

"I'm telling you, it doesn't work," Bess called from the front. She pressed the button, but nothing happened.

The raindrops were falling harder now. They splattered on Nancy's face as she grabbed hold of the vinyl and tugged. The top wouldn't budge. With a sigh, she sat back on her heels. "We'll get soaked."

Bess reached back and held up the two rain slickers. "Not if we drive fast."

"Oh, great." Nancy rolled her eyes as she climbed into the front seat and she and Bess slipped on the slickers. Nancy barely had a chance to fasten her seat belt before Bess hit the gas pedal. The car shot forward, throwing Nancy back against the seat.

"Maybe we can outrun the storm," Bess said.

As they sped along, huge drops of rain pelted the girls' faces and soaked their hair, while the windshield wipers whipped back and forth with an irregular *clunk, clunk.* Nancy was thankful that the slickers kept the rest of them fairly dry. The whole thing was so ridiculous that Nancy had to laugh.

"I think the rental company should refund your money!" she shouted across the seat.

Bess laughed. "I think they should give us hazard pay!"

They reached the drag strip in record time. "I guess everyone else knew it was going to rain," Nancy said as Bess pulled into the nearly empty lot.

Nancy looked at herself in the sideview mirror. Her mascara had formed black smudges under her eyes, and her hair was a tangle of wet, matted strands. "Boy, I'm a mess."

By then the rain had slowed to a drizzle. Bess got out, opened the trunk, and pulled out a folded sheet of plastic. "We can cover the seats with this. Maybe then the car won't turn into a swimming pool while it's sitting here."

"You're really prepared," Nancy commented.

Bess nodded. "Thanks to good old Dad. The rental company won't exchange the car until Monday, so I'm stuck until then."

"It's a good thing my car will be ready late this afternoon," Nancy said, grinning at Bess.

After the girls covered the car, they walked to the pit area and stepped through the gate.

In the gray, misty light, the pit seemed almost menacing. The field was still dotted with an assortment of vehicles, but it looked more like a battlefield after the fight. A dozen or so people were there, checking out tires and tinkering with motors. Except for the pitter-patter of rain, it was quiet.

Nancy spotted Dirk and Jake next to Big D's Dynomite. Jake was drinking from a Styrofoam coffee cup while he watched Dirk tinker with the engine. Both were fairly dry. Nancy guessed they'd sat out the heaviest rain in one of the nearby buildings.

When the guys looked up, Nancy noticed they had dark circles under their eyes, as if they hadn't slept.

"Morning." Dirk nodded at the girls, then gave Bess a smile. "You girls ready to work?

It's tough to scare up a crew on such short notice."

"I take it that means Kitty's still in hiding?" Nancy asked gently.

Dirk traded glances with Jake. "Yeah. We had a long talk with her last night," he told Nancy. "She did say she'd talk to you—later."

Nancy wanted to press him for more information, but she held back. Dirk might decide not to help her at all if she pushed too hard.

All she said was, "I hope it's soon. The police are looking for Kitty, and we can't withhold information from them. It seems Jimmy Sandia had a prior record for auto theft. He worked with a female partner who could have been Kitty."

Dirk and Jake didn't act surprised. "She's laying low because she doesn't want to get nailed for killing Jimmy," Jake explained. "Dirk will take you to her later, when it gets dark." There wasn't a bit of flirtation in his voice now, Nancy noticed. Jake's feelings for Kitty were obviously deeper than Nancy had guessed.

"In the meantime, how about some elbow grease?" Dirk said, clapping his hands together. He handed Nancy and Bess a can of car wax and two clean rags. "I had a good race last night, but the Big D got a little smudged. She'd love a good polishing before my race late this afternoon."

"Sure, I'd love to help," Bess said brightly. Nancy chuckled to herself. She didn't think Bess had ever waxed a car in her life.

The rain had stopped, and the sun was peeking out from behind the clouds. Nancy and Bess shed their slickers and got to work. Nancy caught Bess and Dirk staring at each other a few times. Maybe there was a chance things would work out for them.

At one point Dirk took off to get some water for the engine. Nancy walked over to Jake, who was bent over the Big D's exposed front end.

She didn't want to wait all day to find Kitty. Maybe she could convince Jake to take her there earlier. Besides, she hadn't really talked to him about Jimmy Sandia's murder. If he was close to Kitty, maybe he knew more than he was letting on.

"So where were you yesterday when all the excitement was going on?" Nancy asked lightly.

Jake straightened up and gave her a stony look.

"I already told the cops," Jake told her. "You know, your two buddies."

"Detectives Hawkins and Powderly?" Nancy guessed.

Jake nodded. "They were here nosing around the track this morning." Without another word, he went back to his work. Clearly, he was through talking to Nancy.

With a sigh, Nancy began polishing again.

She was beginning to feel as if she'd never get to the bottom of this case.

"I can't believe how excited I am!" Bess exclaimed. It was late afternoon and she and Nancy were sitting on the hilltop overlooking the track.

The girls had helped Dirk and Jake get the Big D ready all day, stopping only briefly for lunch. Now it was time for the race.

At the starting line, Big D's Dynomite zoomed forward in a burst of speed. In the lane next to it, an orange car did the same.

"They're off!" Nancy cried. She couldn't believe how excited she was.

She frowned a second later when the cars screeched to sudden stops, then backed up to the line again.

"Relax. That's just the burn-out," Bess explained. "They do it to heat up the tires. Gives them better traction for a faster start. These races are so short, they're often won by just a fraction of a second."

Nancy looked at her friend, surprised. "I'm impressed. Where'd you learn all that?"

"Dirk explained it yesterday," Bess said proudly. "He said the cars can go up to a hundred and sixty miles an hour, so the race only lasts a little over eight seconds. There's a light beam that records the times at the finish line."

Nancy looked down at the short track. Chain-link fencing ran along both sides of it, and a huge cornfield bordered the end. A tractor and pesticide sprayer were parked out in the field.

There was a loud roar, and Bess jumped to her feet. "There he goes!"

The Big D shot from the starting line and streaked down the straight track, slightly ahead of the other car. At the finish line, a blinking light in Dirk's lane signaled the end.

"He won!" Nancy exclaimed.

Her cheer died a second later because instead of slowing down, Big D's Dynomite continued to barrel even faster down the asphalt track.

"Something's wrong!" Bess gasped.

Finally the back wheels seemed to lock. But by then the Big D was going so fast, it started to skid sideways. Then the car flew into the air and landed with a crash in the cornfield.

Nancy watched in horror as the Big D zigzagged through the soft dirt, obviously out of control.

"Dirk's not stopping," Bess gasped, clutching Nancy's arm. "He's going to hit that tractor!"

Chapter Eleven

BESS SCREAMED as Dirk's car spun sideways in a spray of dust. The Big D crashed into the wheel of the tractor and jolted to a stop.

As the crowd around her stood up, Nancy took off down the hill. She could hear Bess right behind her.

After racing along the track, Nancy took off into the field. She ran between the rows of young corn plants until she reached the car.

The Big D had swung around so that the driver's door was smashed against the tractor wheel. As Nancy yanked open the passenger door, she saw that Dirk was slumped down in the seat. His hands were cupped around his neck, his eyes shut.

"Dirk!" Nancy touched him lightly on the arm. "Are you all right?"

Opening his eyes, Dirk peered sideways at her. "Man, I don't know. I knocked my head on the steering wheel. My neck really hurts."

"Don't move," Nancy cautioned, sliding into the car. "You may have injured it."

He smiled wanly as Bess stuck her head in the open door beside Nancy's. Jake was right behind her. "That was some finish, huh?"

"Shh," Bess said soothingly. "The rescue squad's on the way. Oh, you poor thing!"

"How does the Big D look?" Dirk asked. "Is my car totaled?"

"Just the side door," Jake assured him. "The dirt slowed you down so the impact wasn't as bad as it could've been. What happened anyway?"

"My front brakes didn't work. It felt as if the brake line snapped." Dirk grimaced and added, "I think somebody cut it. It was fine before lunch."

Nancy nodded grimly. "Let me check and see what I can find." She got out, and Bess slid in and took Dirk's hand.

Waving urgently, Nancy motioned to the emergency vehicle that was pulling up. Two paramedics jumped out, carrying medical bags. As they reached the car, Nancy and Jake walked to the front of the Big D.

Crouching down, they looked at the area near the left wheel. Brake fluid was everywhere. When Nancy inspected the line, she saw that it had been sliced. "Dirk was right," she said grimly.

"Check this out," Jake added, tapping one end of the severed brake line. Looking more closely, Nancy saw that the end had only been sliced partially through. The rest was frayed, as if it had snapped from pressure.

"Whoever did this only cut part of the way through the line," Jake explained. "That way the brakes would hold during the burn-out, then snap when Dirk tried to stop at the finish line. That's when there's a lot more pressure on the brakes."

Nancy straightened up just as the paramedics lifted Dirk out the passenger door and onto a stretcher. A protective collar had been placed around his neck. She and Jake walked next to the stretcher on one side, and Bess was on the other.

"You were right about the brakes," Nancy whispered to Dirk. "Who could have done it?"

"Kitty." Dirk's voice was a whisper.

"Kitty did it?"

He frowned. "No. *Ask* Kitty."

"But where is she?" Nancy leaned closer to hear the answer.

"She'll find you."

As the paramedics slid the stretcher into the emergency van, Bess said firmly, "I want to ride with him."

"Good idea," Nancy agreed. "I'll meet you at the hospital as soon as I can."

"Right." Bess fished in her purse for her car keys and handed them to Nancy. Then she climbed into the van and sat next to Dirk.

Nancy watched as the van drove away, siren blaring. When she looked back at Jake, he was studying her. "Why would somebody want to hurt Dirk?" he asked.

"That's what I'd like to know," said Nancy. "My guess is that someone thinks you and Dirk know too much. This was his—or her—way of warning you to keep your information to yourself. Or maybe they wanted you both away from the track."

Nancy hadn't mentioned Kitty by name, but she could see that Jake got her point. He smoothed back his hair with a nervous gesture. After a long pause, he said, "Kitty did tell us some stuff last night—stuff I didn't know about." He frowned. "I thought I was dating a hotshot mechanic. I was shocked when I found out she and Jimmy Sandia were stealing cars."

So Kitty *was* Jimmy's partner, Nancy thought. But was she a murderer, too? "What did she say happened in the shed yesterday?" Nancy asked.

Jake shrugged. "She just said she'd arranged to meet Jimmy there after she overheard you and Bess talking about a guy with a red ponytail. But she says she didn't kill him," he added quickly.

"I'm not so sure about that," Nancy told him. "The police were ready to close in on Jimmy. Kitty might've been afraid he'd turn her in. And it looks as if she's the only suspect the police have."

Jake leveled a serious gaze at Nancy. "That's why she's so scared," he explained. "She thinks she was set up."

"Who would set her up?" Nancy asked.

"I don't know," he answered, holding up his hands in a helpless gesture. "I think that's what she wants to tell you."

Just then a tow truck rattled to the end of the track and honked. Jake and Nancy moved away from the Big D.

"I know you're not supposed to see Kitty till later, but . . ." He took a deep breath, then said, "In the pit area there's a big dual-wheel pickup hooked to a long, enclosed trailer. It's used for hauling cars. The trailer has Tiny's Mean Machine written on it. That's Tiny's rig. He'll tell you where Kitty is."

"Tiny?" Nancy asked, raising an eyebrow.

"You'll know him when you see him," Jake told her. "After I get Dirk's car taken care of, I'm going to the hospital." Giving Nancy a smile, he said, "Thanks. And good luck."

I'll need it, Nancy thought, crossing slowly toward the pit area. There were still so many unanswered questions—such as who had sabotaged Dirk's car? And who on the police force was trying to sabotage the auto theft investigation? There was some connection she was missing. Nancy could just feel it, but couldn't bring it into focus.

One thing was clear: Dirk wasn't a suspect anymore. He wouldn't have caused his own accident. Also she couldn't imagine Jake doing something to hurt his own brother. Still, Nancy thought, Jake *was* involved with Kitty. . . .

She slowed her steps, wondering if she should call Detective Quinones, then quickly decided against it. If Kitty smelled a cop, she'd never come out of hiding. Nancy decided to take the chance that Jake and Kitty were telling the truth.

But that didn't mean she wouldn't be careful.

A cool wind whipped through the area, and goose bumps prickled Nancy's arms. With Bess gone, she suddenly felt all alone. The pit area was full of people now, but no one she knew she could trust.

Nancy's senses were extra alert as she approached Tiny's truck. The enclosed trailer, which was hooked up to it, was big—large enough to hold two cars.

She walked around to the back of the trailer. The ramp was down, and the heavy metal doors were open, but a canvas tarp hung over the entrance so Nancy couldn't see inside. With a deep breath, she walked up the ramp, pulled the tarp aside, and stuck her head into the dark trailer.

In the next instant, a hand was clapped over Nancy's mouth and a strong arm had circled around her chest.

Nancy tried to scream, but it came out a muffled grunt. Then she felt herself being hoisted into the air. Kicking her feet, she tried to free herself, but the person's hold only tightened. Nancy's heart flip-flopped. She was trapped and no one knew where she was!

"Hold still. I'm not gonna hurt you," a man's voice said gruffly.

"Thanks, Tiny," a softer voice spoke up. Nancy strained to look through the dark. It was Kitty Lambert. The brunette was sitting cross-legged on a bed of blankets at the front of the darkened trailer. A half-eaten sandwich, a bag of potato chips, and a bottle of soda were next to her.

Tiny gently set Nancy down next to the blankets. Then he stood protectively over Kitty. Nancy's eyes had adjusted to the dark and now recognized the huge man she'd seen Kitty talking to the day before. He was wearing oil-stained coveralls, and his head had been shaved.

"I heard about Dirk," Kitty said quietly, motioning Nancy to sit next to her. Tears filled her eyes. "I'm sorry it's come to this. I hope you can help."

Was that a threat, or a plea for help? Nancy couldn't tell for sure. She nodded calmly, but her heart was still racing. "I'll try. But you'll have to tell me everything."

Kitty sighed and wiped the tears from her eyes. "I didn't kill Jimmy. He was my brother," she said simply.

Nancy's eyes widened in surprise. Her brother! "I'm sorry," she said sincerely. "I had no idea. You have different last names."

"Jimmy was my stepbrother. We didn't tell anyone," Kitty said. "I didn't kill him," she went on, "but I still feel as if it's my fault. I'm the one who got Jimmy into car theft. We both wanted to make it big on the drag-racing circuit—only it takes a lot of money." She sighed. "We got impatient."

"And stealing cars was a way to make big money?" Nancy guessed.

Kitty nodded. "Jimmy made enough to buy the car of his dreams. Then he got careless in Chicago and almost got caught, so we split. River Heights seemed like a perfect place to work. There's a track, and we knew from people in the auto theft business that there was already an established chop shop, too. In fact, they recruited us as soon as we hit town."

"Who's 'they'?" Nancy asked eagerly.

Kitty raised her head, her dark eyes glistening. "I wish I knew. Everything was done over the phone. After we agreed to work for them, a guy would call me and request a certain make and year of car. My job was to locate it."

"Ahhh," Nancy said. "That's why we saw you at the Scene."

"Right. And uh"—lowering her eyes, Kitty hesitated—"I was working that night at the restaurant, too."

"Bess's car?"

"Yeah. They were hot for a Camaro. It was the first one I'd seen all week. I mean, I had no idea it belonged to your friend," Kitty quickly added.

"So you'd scout out the car, then call Jimmy."

Kitty nodded. "Jimmy would steal it, then drive it to an empty warehouse and leave it. He never saw anyone."

This was a very slick, professional operation, Nancy realized.

"I want you to tell all of this to the police," Kitty went on. Seeing Nancy's look of surprise, she said bitterly, "Somebody's framing me for Jimmy's murder. Somebody from the chop shop must have killed him because he bungled the last two jobs and was identified. And now they want me out of the way, too."

"You may be right," Nancy said. She tried to think of some way to figure out who was behind the theft ring. "Where exactly did Jimmy leave the cars?" she asked.

Kitty shook her head helplessly. "I was never there, and I never asked. The less I knew, the better."

Frustrated, Nancy sat down on the blankets. "There has to be some way we can track down these guys."

Kitty thought a minute. "Wait—we did briefly meet one man. He came to the track when Jimmy and I first came to town. He said he knew we'd been involved in a theft ring in Chicago and were we interested in working in River Heights. Of course we played dumb in case he was a cop. But we checked around and found out he was on the level."

"What did he look like?" Nancy asked.

Kitty opened her mouth to answer, then froze as a scraping noise sounded from the outside of the trailer. She jumped to her feet, panicked.

With a finger to his lips, Tiny started toward the tarp. At the same time, it was thrown back and Detectives Hawkins and Powderly stared into the trailer.

Kitty grabbed Nancy's arm. "That's him!" she cried in a low voice. "That's the guy!"

Chapter Twelve

"RUN, KITTY!" Tiny boomed. He launched himself at the two detectives. Arms outstretched, he catapulted through the tarp, knocking Powderly and Hawkins flat onto the outside ramp.

Nancy sprang to her feet, but Kitty already had a lead on her. The brunette ran to the end of the trailer and jumped to the ground. By the time Nancy reached the ramp, Kitty was nowhere in sight.

A moment later Nancy heard the roar of a motor and the squeal of wheels. Kitty had escaped.

With a sigh, Nancy turned back to Tiny and the two detectives, who were grappling on the ground outside the trailer. Even two against one, they barely managed to subdue the big man.

A shiver raced up Nancy's spine as she watched the detectives.

Hawkins. Powderly. One of them was the man who'd contacted Kitty and Jimmy about joining the theft ring. Whichever officer it was, he wasn't just being paid off to sabotage the police investigation—he was a key player in the auto theft ring.

"You guys are cops?" Tiny was saying as B. D. Hawkins flashed his badge. The big man seemed to be surprised.

"Yeah. And you'd better cooperate," Powderly snapped, "because we've got plenty of questions for you."

Hawkins noticed Nancy just then. "What are *you* doing here?"

Nancy wondered how much she should tell them. It would be better to report to Detective Quinones, but she didn't have much choice. "Kitty wanted to talk to me," she finally said. "She admitted that she worked with Jimmy Sandia, stealing cars, but she said she didn't kill him."

"Yeah, right," Hawkins scoffed. "You knew we were looking for Kitty. Why didn't you tell us where she was? I ought to arrest you for obstructing justice!"

"I didn't know where she was until a few minutes ago," Nancy said calmly. She filled in Hawkins and Powderly about Dirk's accident, and about what the Walters brothers had told her.

"Kitty was in the trailer all day," Tiny spoke up, "so she couldn't have tampered with his car."

"Maybe," Stan Powderly said dubiously. "But even if Kitty *isn't* guilty of murdering her partner, we still need to talk to her. Seems she's the one person who can help us decide who *is* our culprit."

Nancy nodded her head in agreement. "Maybe Tiny can tell us where she went."

Tiny simply shrugged. "Beats me, but she probably got away in a 1988 Thunderbird."

Nancy studied the big man closely. She was almost positive he was lying to the detectives—he was too protective of Kitty to give away the real description of her car. She didn't want the crooked cop to know that, though, so she said nothing.

"Thanks," Detective Powderly told Tiny. "We'll radio that information out." He left for his car.

Hawkins looked suspiciously at Tiny, then at Nancy. "You two better be telling us everything," he growled. Then he stalked off, muttering, "Man, I'm glad my shift is over and I'm headed home."

When the two detectives had driven off, Tiny shook his head. "I don't believe it. One of the guys who Kitty and Jimmy were working for was actually a cop."

"That doesn't mean it's okay for Kitty to run from the police," Nancy said firmly. She wrote her number down on a piece of paper, then pulled out Detective Quinones's card and copied his number down, too. "You tell her to call me, or Raul Quinones," she instructed, handing Tiny the piece of paper. "He's the detective I'm reporting to. If she turns herself in, he'll make sure she's all right."

A few minutes later, as Nancy trudged toward the concession stand, she realized how exhausted and hungry she was. It was almost seven, and she hadn't eaten since lunch. First she wanted to get to a phone and contact Detective Quinones. He needed to know about how Kitty had fingered one of his detectives.

When she reached the concession stand, she went to the phone booth and left a message for Quinones that she had called and would try again from the hospital. Then, after grabbing a hot dog, she drove to the River Heights Hospital.

A nurse directed Nancy down the hall, where Bess greeted her. Dirk was next to her, lying on a gurney next to a door marked X Rays. Nancy was pleased to see that there was color in his face, though he was still wearing a neck brace.

"I guess you're not hurt too badly, if they're leaving you out in the hall," she joked.

Smiling up at her, Dirk said, "The X rays show my neck's still there. I think they're going to let me go home. There aren't any empty rooms, so I'm stuck here until I get the final word."

"Jake just got here, too," Bess told Nancy. "He went to get some sodas. He said he'll drive Dirk home when he's released."

"They ran a bunch of tests," Dirk added. "So far everything looks okay."

"Hey, Nancy." Jake came down the hall holding three cans of soda. "Did you see Kitty?" he asked.

"Yes." Nancy filled them all in on what Kitty had said. She decided not to mention that Kitty had indicated that Hawkins or Powderly was the bad cop. The fewer people who knew about that, the better.

When she'd finished talking, Dirk said, "That still doesn't explain who sabotaged my car."

"I think someone did it both as a warning and a distraction," Nancy explained. "That way he or she could hunt for Kitty unnoticed while we were taking care of you."

"That makes sense," Bess agreed. Her next words were swallowed by a huge yawn.

"You girls must be bushed," Jake said. "I'll take over from here."

Bess reached over and squeezed Dirk's hand. "I'll call your house in the morning," she told him.

"'Bye," Nancy said, waving as she and Bess left.

When they reached the lobby, Nancy headed straight for a phone booth. She dialed

Detective Quinones's home number, but there wasn't an answer.

"That's odd," she said when she hung up. "He's not there, and the dispatcher said he wasn't at the station, either."

"Well, he does have a life," Bess commented. "Maybe he and his family went to the movies."

Nancy reached into her purse for more change. "I'll call the station again and leave another message." This time she told the dispatcher to have Detective Quinones call her at home.

"Come on," Bess said as Nancy hung up. "Let's go home."

They walked out into the chilly night. "You can drive," Bess told Nancy, stepping around to the passenger side of the rental car. "After watching Dirk crash, I'm not too eager to get behind the wheel."

"I don't blame you," said Nancy. Getting in on the driver's side, she started the car and drove from the hospital parking lot.

"That's weird," Nancy murmured as they passed a dark blue sedan parked on the street. "That car looks like the one I saw Detective Hawkins driving the other day—you know, after we made our report at the police station. The car even has a dent in the right front fender."

"Huh? Which car?" Bess asked, turning her head. "It's probably just a coincidence."

Just then Nancy saw the car move like a dark

shadow from its parking space. She slowed in time to see it flick its lights on. When she turned right, the car followed, but at a safe distance.

Instinct told Nancy it was no coincidence. B. D. Hawkins was tailing them. "We're being followed," she told Bess.

Bess swung around in her seat. "You mean Detective Hawkins? Why would *he* follow us?"

Nancy told Bess about Kitty's reaction to seeing Powderly and Hawkins at the trailer.

Bess's mouth fell open. "You mean, *he's* the bad cop?" she asked. "I should have known. He's always been so unwilling to help us."

"We don't know for sure that Hawkins is the bad cop. But if he is, maybe he thinks we know where Kitty is," Nancy said, thinking out loud. "Or maybe he's afraid we might know too much."

"W-what should we do?" Bess asked, her voice trembling.

Nancy knit her brow in concentration. "We could just drive home and lay low," she said. "On the other hand, maybe we can outfox Hawkins and find out for sure if he is the crooked cop."

She turned to grin at Bess. "I think I've got an idea that might just work. We'll stop for burgers, and after that we're going to lose him. I'm going to pick up my car at the garage. The owner said it's ready to go. Then I'll follow *him.*"

"What are you talking about?" Bess asked, as if Nancy had lost her mind.

Nancy laughed. "Trust me."

A few minutes later Nancy pulled into the lot of a fast-food restaurant, and the girls ordered from the drive-through window. While they waited, Nancy checked around for Hawkins. There he was. He'd pulled into a vacant spot.

When the food came, Nancy drove toward the garage where she'd had the Mustang repaired. When she was a few blocks away, she suddenly took a sharp right, sped through a narrow alley, and came out on a busy street.

"Whoa!" called Bess, grabbing onto her seat. "I hope you know what you're doing."

"We lost him for a second, but I want him to find us again," Nancy said, glancing in her rearview mirror. "The garage is the next right. I'm going to pull up and jump out. Then you drive back onto Main Street, where we lost him. Let's hope Hawkins spots the convertible again and follows you."

Bess gave Nancy another questioning look. "What about you?"

"I'm going to follow *him* in my car."

"This sounds like something they do in gangster movies," Bess said. "Are you sure it's going to work?"

"No," Nancy said with a laugh, "but we can give it a try."

"I'm game." Bess got ready to scoot into the driver's seat. "Just be careful!"

Nancy turned right into the garage, braked, and jumped out. Bess pulled the door shut. Speeding up, she turned left at the end of the lot.

Jogging over to the Mustang, Nancy unlocked it and climbed in. It started with a wonderful roar. She flicked on the lights and started after Bess. When she turned onto Main Street a minute later, she spotted Bess's rental car a block ahead of hers—and B. D. Hawkins's car was two cars behind it!

Perfect, she thought. The plan is working.

Nancy followed at a distance. When Bess got to her house, Hawkins parked about a block away. Nancy quickly pulled up next to the curb several houses down.

Hawkins sat watching the Marvins' house for an hour. Then, when all the lights were out, he started his car again. Nancy checked her watch, yawning. It was late, but when she began to tail Hawkins, she forgot how tired she was.

She followed the dark blue sedan to the main highway. When Hawkins got off at the industrial section of town, Nancy had a feeling she knew where he was going. Her heartbeat quickened and her palms began to sweat as he turned down the same dead end street where Jimmy Sandia had driven the stolen Camaro.

It was too good to be true. He was leading her right to the chop shop.

Chapter Thirteen

FLICKING OFF HER LIGHTS, Nancy just turned into the street and stopped. Hawkins's car was parked in front of R. H. Shipping—the same building where the Mustang had crashed after the run-in with the car carrier.

The area was dark and deserted, as Nancy would expect late on a Saturday night. She could see that Hawkins wasn't in his car. He must have gone into the warehouse already. That confirmed her suspicions—only someone working with the auto theft ring would have a key to get in. He certainly wasn't on official police business—Nancy had heard him say his shift was over when he left the track.

Scanning the front of the warehouse, she saw that there were no windows and only one entrance except for a garage door, which was closed.

Nancy knew she should call Detective Quinones right away and let him handle things from now on. First, though, she just wanted to check inside Hawkins's car. There was always a chance that he had been careless and left some clue.

Moving as quietly as possible, she crept up to the detective's car. When she peeked in, she could see Hawkins's leather jacket hanging over the back of the seat.

She pressed the door handle and was surprised to find it unlocked. Why would he be so careless? she wondered. Unless it was on purpose. Maybe he knew she'd been tailing him, and this was a trap.

There was only one way to find out. Carefully, Nancy squeezed through the open door and sat in the driver's seat. She decided to start with the leather jacket. Searching the pockets, she found a wad of lint and some gum wrappers.

"What's this?" Nancy murmured, noticing a white strip of paper mixed in with the wrappers. It had been torn in half, but she clearly recognized it—it was a strip of evidence tape!

Nancy pulled her flashlight from her purse and shined it on the torn tape. Hawkins was printed on it, along with a date, which had been two days earlier, she realized. The night of the stakeout at the Scene.

This had to be the tape used to tag the bag

with the slim jim in it! So Hawkins was the person who opened the evidence bag, wiped the prints off the slim jim, then rebagged it using new tape to seal the top. He'd probably been in a hurry and stuck the scrap from the old evidence tape in his jacket pocket.

Nancy shuddered. B. D. Hawkins was definitely the bad cop—and quite possibly Jimmy Sandia's murderer!

Trying to ignore the prickly feeling at the back of her neck, Nancy slipped the tape into her purse. Then she stuffed the wrappers back in Hawkins's jacket and rearranged it on the seat. After creeping out of the car, she ran back to the Mustang and started it. She had to get out of there—fast. A deserted street in the middle of the night was the last place she wanted to meet B. D. Hawkins.

On the drive home Nancy kept checking her rearview mirror. No one was tailing her. Only when she was safely inside her house did she breathe a sigh of relief. As she leaned against the front door, her gaze fell on a note from Hannah that was sitting on the front table. It read, "Call Detective Quinones at home."

Nancy took the steps up to her room two at a time and dialed his number on her phone. He answered on the first ring.

"Where have you been?" he asked after Nancy identified herself. "I've been calling every half-hour since I got your message. Your housekeeper was tired of being waked up."

"I've been tailing Detective Hawkins," Nancy explained. She went on to tell him about Kitty's reaction to seeing Powderly and Hawkins that afternoon, and about following Hawkins to the chop shop.

After a long pause Detective Quinones asked, "You're *sure* it was the chop shop?"

"Not positive," Nancy admitted, "but I know it was Hawkins's car. It had his jacket in it, and when I searched his pockets I found—"

Suddenly Nancy hesitated. Maybe she shouldn't mention the evidence tape. She'd let Quinones identify it himself. Then he could decide if it implicated Hawkins or not. "I found something I want you to see."

"Well, it'll have to wait till morning," Detective Quinones said. "Homicide just called with something I have to check on right away. I'll meet you at the station tomorrow morning at eight-thirty."

"All right," Nancy agreed. "See you then."

"I'm exhausted," Bess said when Nancy picked her up at home. "I didn't get to bed last night until after one."

Nancy smiled at her friend. "I'm kind of beat, too."

"Oh—Dirk asked if we could pick him up on our way," Bess added. "I told him about Hawkins following us, and he said he wants to come to the police station, too," Bess told Nancy. "He said something about finding the creeps that did in the Big D."

"I guess that means Dirk's feeling better," Nancy said with a laugh.

"He's really upset about his car, though," Bess said. She let out a sigh. "I can't help thinking about the Camaro, too. I know it's probably in a million pieces by now, but I keep hoping we'll find it."

Dirk was waiting on the porch when the girls arrived at his house. He was sitting on the steps, the protective collar still around his neck.

"How are you?" Nancy asked him.

"Great," he replied. "I don't feel any pain, but the doctor told me to leave this on for a few days just to be safe."

Fifteen minutes later the three teenagers entered the auto theft office at the police station. Stan Powderly was there and greeted them with a tired smile. His suit was rumpled, and two half-empty containers of coffee were on his desk.

"Change of plans. Raul called about half an hour ago," he said, getting up to close the outside door. "We don't need anyone overhearing this," he added in a low voice.

"Where's Detective Quinones?" Nancy asked, as she, Bess, and Dirk sat down. She was instantly alert. She didn't like the idea that he wasn't there. She also didn't want to tell Powderly about the evidence tape before showing it to Quinones.

Powderly was grim. "Raul's still over at the garage at the racetrack. Early this morning, homicide called him. Seems they found something that—" He paused, a frown of uncertainty on his face. "I guess I can tell you this," he finally said. "Raul confided in me that you were working on the case, Nancy. Anyway, they found something that definitely implicates Detective Hawkins in the murder of Jimmy Sandia."

Bess drew in her breath sharply. "So we were right!" she exclaimed softly.

"What did they find?" Nancy asked.

"Homicide found a partial boot print in the dirt near the tractor where Jimmy was murdered. They matched it to Hawk's cowboy boot."

"What does that prove?" Dirk wanted to know. "I mean, Hawkins *is* part of the investigating team. It makes sense that his print would be there."

Nancy snapped her fingers. "But he didn't show up until *after* the homicide people had sealed off the scene," she said, remembering. "By then Detective Quinones had everyone stay clear so that they wouldn't mess up evidence."

"Wow!" Bess exclaimed.

"Yeah, wow," Stan echoed dryly. "And all this time I thought B.D. was working *with* us."

"So why would Hawkins murder Jimmy Sandia?" Nancy asked. She still didn't want Powderly to know how much she'd already learned.

Stan gave a tired sigh, shaking his head.

"Raul told me this morning that someone on the force is working with the auto thieves," he explained. "Right away I thought of Hawk. He hasn't been himself lately—as if he's not part of the team anymore. Plus he's so cocky. I bet he thinks he can do it all—even break the law—and not get caught."

So Detective Quinones had finally confided in Powderly, Nancy thought. The boot print must have made him certain that the bad cop was Hawkins.

"What are you and Detective Quinones going to do now?" Bess asked, twisting a strand of blond hair between her fingers.

"Well, we've cooked up a plan to catch Hawkins in action," Powderly replied. He fixed each of the teenagers with a serious look, then said, "And you three are going to be part of it."

"Great!" Dirk sat up, excited. "Does it involve some fast driving?"

Shooting Dirk a stern glance, Bess said, "Hey! You just got out of the hospital, remember?"

"It's nothing that exciting," Detective Powderly said quickly. "Nancy, your job will be to call Hawkins and tell him you've located the warehouse. Tell him you can't find Raul or me, and ask him to meet you there."

"Where? I mean, we don't know exactly which warehouse it is," Nancy said.

The detective gave a small smile. "I had the uniformed cops keep an eye on the street where you and Bess followed Jimmy Sandia. They've reported some unusual activity that narrows it down to R. H. Shipping."

"That makes sense," Bess commented. "That's where those goons were on the loading dock."

Nancy nodded. So far the plan sounded solid.

"Nancy, you can tell Hawkins that Kitty Lambert told you R. H. Shipping is where Jimmy took the stolen cars," Powderly continued. "That should convince him to meet you there."

"Sounds good," said Nancy. "What should we do when we get there?"

Detective Powderly picked up a small tape recorder from his desk and handed it to her. "First of all you'll be carrying this. You need to get Hawk to confess to something incriminating. Raul and I figured he'd tell you more than he'd ever confess to us. So play it by ear. Raul and I and several other plainclothes officers will be hiding nearby, so there's nothing to worry about."

"Wow. Cops and robbers," Dirk put in excitedly. "Sounds good to me."

"Me, too," Bess said. "I can't wait to see Hawkins and his chop shop buddies get caught. This'll show him that nobody steals my car and gets away with it."

Stan laughed. "Leave the rough stuff to the police, Ms. Marvin. You just need to get Hawk to confess something that will lead us to the others. As far as he goes, the boot print and scrap of evidence tape will put him away for a *long* time."

Nancy frowned as the detective's words sank in, reverberating in her mind.

Evidence tape. She hadn't told *anyone* about the tape. There was only one way Detective Powderly could know about it. And that was if *he'd* been the one to take the tape off the evidence bag and plant the tape in B.D.'s car. The bad cop on the force wasn't B. D. Hawkins—it was Stan Powderly!

Chapter Fourteen

NANCY'S MIND began to whirl. She never would have believed that Stan Powderly could be so devious. He had set up Hawkins to take the fall for everything—including murder.

Thinking back to the night before, Nancy realized that it was possible that Powderly, and not Hawkins, had been behind the wheel of Hawkins's car. If that was true, maybe Powderly knew that she followed him—right to the warehouse.

Maybe that was why it had been so easy to get into the car. Stan had *wanted* her to find the evidence tape, figuring that she'd report it to Quinones. But what about the boot print homicide had found in the garage? Had Powderly planted that, too?

Suddenly Nancy felt as if a huge weight were pressing down on her shoulders. Powderly was setting them *all* up now, with his warehouse plan—she knew it. One wrong move could put them all in jeopardy. The only thing on their side was the fact that Stan didn't know she was onto him.

"Nancy, did you hear what I said?" Bess asked, drawing Nancy's attention back to the little cubicle.

"What? Oh—sorry, Bess," Nancy said quickly, not daring to look at Powderly.

"I was saying, we'd better get a move on," Bess told her. "We've got a criminal to catch!"

"That's for sure," Nancy murmured.

Powderly lifted the phone receiver. "Sunday is Hawk's day off," he said, "so he'll be home. Remember what you should say?"

Nancy nodded. "That Kitty told us where the warehouse was and he's to meet us there."

"Right," Stan said approvingly. "And make sure you mention that you couldn't find Raul or me."

Nancy tapped her foot nervously as Stan punched in the phone number. He handed her the receiver as a young child answered the phone with a loud hello. "Daddy, it's for you!" Nancy heard the boy call.

"Yeah." Hawkins's voice was curt.

"Hi. It's Nancy Drew," she said over the line. Then she told him the story Powderly had concocted. "I wasn't able to get a hold of Detective Quinones or Powderly, but I left messages," she finished. "If you can meet us there, we'll show you which building it is."

There was a short pause before Hawkins said, "All right. I can make it in twenty minutes."

When Nancy hung up, Dirk was already springing from his chair. "Let's roll!" he exclaimed.

"And find my car!" Bess added.

Nancy pasted an enthusiastic smile on her face. After all, she didn't want Powderly to suspect anything.

Stan clapped his hands together. "You guys make a good team. I'll round up the other cops and wait for Raul. When he's done at the track, he'll stop at the judge's to get a search warrant." He checked his watch. "It's eight-forty. Be at the warehouse at five of nine. Hawk should be there by then."

While he talked, Nancy frowned in concentration. Everything he said made so much sense. He'd obviously thought out his plan carefully. Even his reasons why Detective Quinones wasn't here were logical. If he hadn't made the slip about the evidence tape, Nancy wouldn't have been the least bit suspicious.

Powderly shook their hands as they left. "Good luck, team," he said.

Nancy was silent as she, Bess, and Dirk walked to the Mustang. Bess slid into the back seat behind Nancy, then Dirk got in the front passenger seat.

"Okay, Nan. 'Fess up," Bess said, leaning

forward and resting her arms on the back of Nancy's seat. "I can tell you're worried about something. You've hardly said a word in the past ten minutes."

"Do you think B.D. might be dangerous?" Dirk asked. "Don't tell me the famous detective sees a glitch in Stan's plan?"

"More like she smells a big rat," Nancy said. "You guys, I never told Detective Quinones about finding the evidence tape. I was going to show it to him this morning and get his reaction."

For a moment Bess and Dirk stared at her blankly. Then Dirk said slowly, "So what you're saying is, if Powderly knew about the tape it means he must've put it there himself."

"You mean *Stan's* the bad cop?" Bess asked in disbelief.

Nancy nodded. "Looks like it. We've got to find a phone and contact Detective Quinones," she said, starting the car. "B. D. Hawkins is being set up, and so are we."

Moments later Nancy spotted a pay phone at a gas station. Pulling in, she grabbed some change from her purse and jogged over to the phone. Since she hadn't seen Quinones at the police station she decided to try him at his house.

Relief flooded Nancy when the detective answered. "Detective Quinones? This is Nancy," she said into the receiver. "Has Stan Powderly talked to you this morning?"

"Yeah. He said you called in and postponed

our meeting until ten o'clock. I'll be a little late. I have to stop back at the drag strip."

"Is that about the boot print?" Nancy asked.

"How did you know?"

Quickly Nancy filled him in on what had just happened. When she was done, she heard a low whistle over the line.

"Wow," Detective Quinones said. "Stan Powderly! I never would've guessed." Then his voice turned serious. "He's obviously willing to do anything to save his own hide. I'll radio for backup to meet me at the warehouse. I want you kids to stay away," he said firmly. "Stan could be very dangerous."

When Nancy hung up, she breathed a sigh of relief. It was nice to have the police step in. As she got back into the car, though, another thought occurred to her.

"Oh, no," she said in a low voice.

"You didn't get Detective Quinones?" Bess asked worriedly.

"Oh, I got him. He's going right to the warehouse, but who knows how long it will take him to get there." Checking her watch, Nancy saw that it was almost nine.

Dirk turned to Nancy, a worried look on his face. "But Hawkins is supposed to meet us there any minute."

Nancy nodded grimly. "Which means he'll walk right into whatever trap Powderly's cooked up." She started the Mustang and pulled out of the gas station. "We've got to warn him!"

Nancy made it to the warehouse in record time. Detective Hawkins's empty car was already parked in front of R. H. Shipping. Nancy stopped the Mustang beside it, then checked the loading dock and garage door.

"I don't see anyone," she said. "But the garage door's open. Hawkins must have gone in already."

Following Nancy's gaze, Dirk said, "Maybe Powderly's in there, too. Just because his car isn't around doesn't mean he's not."

"That's right. We'd better be extra careful," Nancy warned. Opening her door, she swung her legs out.

"Uh—are we going in there?" Bess asked in a worried voice.

Nancy tossed the keys to Bess. "I'm going in. You guys wait for Quinones. He should be here soon."

"No way!" Dirk opened his door and jumped out. "You're not going in there alone."

Nancy could see that he wasn't going to back down. "Okay," she agreed. "Bess, if we're not out in ten minutes, take off and find the police."

"Good luck!" Bess said, flashing them the thumbs-up sign.

Nancy and Dirk eased up the loading ramp and slipped into the building through the open garage door. Except for the light streaming in the open doorway, the warehouse was dark.

She and Dirk paused to let their eyes adjust. Finally they could see that they were inside a huge, windowless room. Against the back wall, boxes were piled to the ceiling. A large freight elevator was built into the right wall. A freight elevator to where? Nancy wondered for a second before she remembered Hawkins. There was no sign of him or anyone else.

"I wonder where Hawkins is," Nancy whispered. She pointed to a door with a window about halfway down the right wall. "Maybe that's an office. I'll check."

She strode across the room and tried the handle. The door was locked. Pulling her penlight from her purse, she shined the beam through the window. "Nothing much in there," she murmured. "Just a desk and some file cabinets." She resolved to check back for information about the chop shop. Right now, her priority was to warn Detective Hawkins.

When she turned around, she saw Dirk standing by the boxes piled to the ceiling against the rear wall.

"Someone's been painting in here," he whispered as Nancy joined him. "I can smell it."

"You're right!" Nancy whispered back, sniffing the air and trying to locate its source. "Maybe there's something behind these," she suggested, tapping the boxes. "It looks as though they're stacked several deep."

They began moving boxes. When they had cleared a space, Nancy flashed her light into it. The beam illuminated a narrow metal staircase that led upward into the ceiling.

She gave a low whistle. "They sure didn't want anyone to find this."

"What do you think's up there?" Dirk asked.

"Only one way to find out," Nancy said. Meeting Dirk's gaze, she asked, "Ready?"

He took a deep breath. "Ready."

They squeezed between the boxes and climbed the steps, Dirk leading the way. When they emerged onto the second floor, Nancy's mouth fell open.

Skylights in the roof illuminated a huge room filled with cars in various stages of being painted or dismantled. One corner of the room was heaped with parts and shipping boxes. Another corner held an array of paint cans and tools. The freight elevator opening was in the side wall.

"Wow," Nancy exclaimed softly. "I'd say we found the chop shop."

Chapter Fifteen

"WHAT A SETUP," Nancy said, walking over to a car that was taped for painting. "All they have to do is grind out the VIN on the newer ones, repaint them, and sell them."

She turned to take in the rest of the room. As the floor below, there were no people. "I wonder where Hawkins is?" she asked anxiously. "We need to get out of here before Powderly comes."

Dirk didn't hear Nancy. He was busy picking up a spray gun. A canister of paint was attached to the gun's handle, and a long hose led to an air compressor. He idly flicked on the compressor. "It takes about ten minutes for these babies to warm up," he said. "But when they do, they can change the color of a car in an hour or two."

"Come on," Nancy urged. "Let's get back outside and wait for Quinones."

They were back at the steps when Nancy heard a low moan coming from behind a pile of shipping boxes in the middle of the room. Dirk's eyes opened wide. Nancy nodded toward the boxes, and the two crept over.

Nancy saw something move beneath the junk as they approached. Bending down, she pulled a box away, revealing an arm in a brown leather jacket. "Help me, Dirk," Nancy said. "Hawkins is under these boxes."

They pulled the empty boxes off the detective. When he was finally uncovered, they helped him to a sitting position. His mouth had been taped shut, and his hands and legs were bound together with rope. Blood was dripping from an ugly-looking cut at the back of his head.

"You're hurt!" Nancy exclaimed. Squatting down next to the detective, she inspected the wound more closely. "At least it's not very deep."

"Here, take this," said Dirk. He pulled a handkerchief from his pocket and gave it to Nancy, who tied it around Hawkins's head. Then she peeled back a corner of the tape across his mouth and was just ready to rip it off.

"I wouldn't do that if I were you," a voice said behind them.

Nancy whirled around. Stan Powderly stood over her, a gun in his hand.

"If I'd wanted Hawk to talk, I wouldn't have taped his mouth shut," Powderly went on.

"But he's hurt," she protested.

"Obviously not hurt enough," said Powderly. "I thought I hit him hard enough to put him out for good. Too bad your head's so hard, Hawk. Now you'll have to watch."

Dirk eyed Powderly uneasily. "What are you going to do to us?" he asked.

Powderly just grinned. For the first time Nancy could see the evil in his face. With his pink cheeks and round belly, he looked like a sinister clown.

"He's not going to do anything," Nancy retorted. "Bess will tell Detective Quinones where we are. He should be here any second."

At that, Stan chuckled. "Your little friend isn't going to save you."

He stepped aside as two men came up the steps, holding a struggling Bess. Like B. D. Hawkins, her mouth had been taped. Nancy recognized the craggy face of the driver who'd nearly run them down with the car carrier. The other guy was the blond man who'd been on the loading dock that same day.

"Now that they've seen her, tie her up downstairs," Powderly ordered the goons. "I don't want any chance of her helping her friends."

"You're hurting her!" Dirk growled, lunging forward.

"Don't move!" Stan ordered, swinging his gun at Dirk. "Or I'll blow you all away."

Dirk stopped in his tracks. His gaze locked on Bess's as he helplessly watched the two thugs drag her back down the steps.

"As for the great Detective Quinones," Stan continued, "he's going to be hunting through a warehouse at the end of the street, where I parked your Mustang and B.D.'s car."

"Pretty clever," Nancy said, rising slowly to her feet. "But then I knew you'd have to be clever in order to kill Jimmy Sandia and frame your own partner."

Detective Powderly glared at her. "Too bad I had to kill Sandia, but you'd fingered him. It would have only been a matter of time before the cops would have caught him. And as for Hawk—well, since Kitty looks innocent of Jimmy's murder, I had to pin it on somebody."

Hawkins was glaring at his partner, but the tape prevented him from saying anything.

Chuckling to himself, Powderly went on. "But it worked out great. Now Kitty's the only one who can link me to the auto theft ring. And soon the beautiful Ms. Lambert will be killed resisting arrest."

"You wouldn't dare," Dirk said hotly.

"Oh, wouldn't I?" Stan retorted. He became deadly serious as he added, "Now I want you to tie up your boyfriend, Ms. Drew." He waved them toward the freight elevator. "There's some rope over there."

Dirk started over, Nancy next to him. As she

turned, Nancy reached into her jacket pocket and clicked on the tape recorder.

"Don't bother taping this, Ms. Drew," Powderly told her. "We're torching the whole place. All the evidence will be gone. Now that the police have an idea of where this chop shop is, we've got to start all over in a different city."

"But what about these cars and your equipment?" Nancy asked.

"It's cheaper just to replace all of it," Powderly explained with a shrug. "Now quit stalling and tie up your boyfriend."

Dirk put his hands together and held them out to Nancy. When he did, he nodded his head ever so slightly toward the spray gun. Nancy realized that the compressor was still on. Maybe she could use the gun somehow. But how?

"So tell me, Stan. How did you get involved with the auto theft ring?" Nancy asked, trying to buy some time. She moved as slowly as she dared as she looped the rope around Dirk's wrists.

"Easy. I busted a kid stealing cars several months ago, and he led me right to R. H. Shipping. Then I politely informed the head of the ring that either he paid me off, or I turned them all in. You can imagine his decision. My payoffs were so lucrative, I decided to get in on the operation."

Nancy couldn't believe Stan Powderly's

smug attitude. He was actually proud to be a crooked cop! It made her sick.

Powderly waved his gun around the shop as he continued explaining. "Somebody else did all the dirty work. I was just a middle man. My job was to tell Kitty what kind of car was needed."

"So you started leaking information about the police investigation to the people at the chop shop, so they could avoid being caught," Nancy guessed.

"Right. Being on the police force was perfect. Handy for finding new recruits for stealing cars, too. Now do his feet."

Dirk obediently sat on the floor, leaning against the wall. If only she had a diversion, Nancy thought, some way to take Stan's attention.

"How did you manage to frame Hawkins?" she asked, trying to remain calm. The younger detective was still sitting bound on the floor, leaning awkwardly against the boxes. His angry gaze was fixed unwaveringly on Stan Powderly.

"That was easy," said Powderly. "Wiping off the prints was just a matter of breaking into the evidence room. And good old Hawk—he's arrogant but gullible. He lent me his car so I could tail you and plant the evidence tape. I made it pretty obvious that I was following you, figuring that a hot young *detective* like yourself would try to turn the tables on me."

Nancy didn't miss his sneer as he said the word *detective,* but she said nothing.

"Lucky for me, Hawk left his boots in the car," Powderly went on. "That gave me the idea of framing him for Sandia's murder."

Nancy tied one last knot, then stood up. "Sounds like you've got everything covered," she said, pretending to be impressed.

"Yeah—and it was fun." Detective Powderly leered at them. "I even got to dress up like the other grease monkeys at the track, and hang around until I got the chance to kill Jimmy Sandia."

"Then *you* must be the one who cut the brake line on my car," Dirk said angrily.

Powderly nodded. "Right before the race, when you and Ms. Marvin were exchanging good luck smooches, and Ms. Drew was off being a detective somewhere. My plan was to divert attention away from the pit so I could find Kitty Lambert. Didn't work out that way, though."

"You creep," Dirk said. He struggled to stand up, but Powderly swung his gun around to point at him.

"Sit down," Powderly ordered.

In that split second, his attention was diverted. Nancy knew it was now or never.

Diving for the spray gun, she whipped it around and pulled the trigger. Blue paint spurted into Stan Powderly's face. With a scream, he threw up his hands to guard his eyes.

At the same time Dirk launched himself into the back of Powderly's knees. The detective fell backward on top of Dirk, but managed to keep a grip on his gun.

Nancy aimed the stream of spray at Powderly again. This time he managed to lurch backward, just out of reach.

"Nice try, Ms. Drew," Stan said, wiping the paint from his eyes. He stood up, his gun pointed at Nancy's head. "Too bad you didn't succeed, because now I'm through fooling around."

Pulling a cigarette lighter from his pocket, he flicked it open. A blue flame shot into the air. "With all the paint and thinner in here, this place will go up like a torch—with all of you in it!"

Chapter Sixteen

"YOU MUST BE pretty desperate to kill all of us," Nancy said in as calm a voice as she could muster.

"Not desperate. Smart," said Powderly. He started to lower the flame of the lighter toward a cardboard box.

Suddenly there was a crash above them. Nancy raised her head in time to see Raul Quinones drop in from the skylight above.

"What—?" Powderly began. As Quinones landed on his feet on the roof of a car, Powderly quickly flicked off the lighter and once again aimed his gun at Nancy.

At the same time, Quinones drew his gun and ordered, "Drop the gun, Stan."

"I'm not the one you want, Raul," Powderly

said smoothly. "Hawk's your man. These kids were in on the auto theft ring, too."

"Don't believe him," Nancy said to Detective Quinones, trying not to think about the gun pointed at her head. "He was going to set the whole place on fire, with us in it."

"She's crazy." Stan glowered at Nancy. "They decided to work with Hawkins. I caught them painting cars."

"Cut the double-talk, Stan," Quinones said firmly. "It's over. We caught your two goons trying to make a run for it. Even if they won't testify against you, I'm sure Ms. Drew and her friends will."

Stan's eyes narrowed. "You'd take their word over mine?"

"That's right," said Quinones. "Now drop it."

"Never." Stan pressed his gun barrel against Nancy's temple. "Go ahead and shoot me, but the lovely Ms. Drew will die, too."

Nancy's heart was pounding. She knew Detective Quinones didn't have a choice. He'd never risk her life. He lowered his gun without hesitating.

There *had* to be a way, Nancy thought desperately. Her eyes darted quickly around. If she could only distract Powderly . . .

When her gaze landed on B. D. Hawkins, Nancy noticed that he was looking at her. He was still leaning against the boxes in the middle of the room. With a secret wink at Nancy, he began to thrash his body from side to side.

"Knock it off!" Stan shouted, whirling toward Hawkins.

In that second Nancy lashed out with a chop to Powderly's wrist. The gun flew from his hand, skittering across the floor. Before Powderly could recover it, Raul Quinones jumped from the roof of the car, raced over, and landed a punch on Powderly's jaw.

Powderly crumpled backward with a cry. By the time he looked up again, Quinones's gun was trained on him. "You're under arrest, Stan."

As if on cue two other officers raced up the metal staircase. Nancy recognized one of them as Officer Jackson, who immediately twisted Powderly's hands behind his back and handcuffed them. The other officer hurried over to B. D. Hawkins and began untying him.

"Bess!" Nancy exclaimed, as her friend came up the stairs after the officers. "Are you okay?"

Bess nodded. "I'm really sorry. Powderly's goons sneaked up on me in the car. They had my mouth taped before I even knew what was happening. I'm just lucky those other cops found me tied up downstairs in the office."

"It's not your fault," Nancy reassured her. "Powderly sneaked up on all of us."

Bess shivered as she looked at Detective Powderly. "Boy, am I glad you got him. Those goons said he was going to burn this whole place up."

Just then Bess's gaze landed on Dirk, who

was still tied up next to the elevator. "Dirk!" she cried, rushing over to him. She and Nancy quickly untied him.

As soon as Dirk was free, he enveloped Bess in a big hug. "I'm so glad you're not hurt," he said.

"I'm glad we're *all* not hurt," Bess said, but Nancy noticed a slight blush in her friend's cheeks.

Glancing around at all the parts, Nancy said, "Well, we finally found the chop shop, but I don't see your Camaro anywhere, Bess."

"I guess we were too late," Dirk added. Seeing the disappointment on Bess's face, he took her hand. "Hey, with my contacts, we'll find you a new car in no time. Maybe something as nice as—" His glance fell on a red sports car in the corner. "Something as nice as that baby."

Bess forced a smile. "Okay. It's a deal."

Nancy went over to Detective Hawkins, who was sitting on the floor, rubbing his ankles where they'd been bound.

"I want to apologize for suspecting you," Nancy said. "If you hadn't distracted Powderly, we all could have been in big trouble."

Hawkins held up his hand to quiet her. "I'm the one who should apologize," he said with a smile. "For doubting your abilities. You're one smart detective, Nancy Drew."

As Officer Jackson and the other officer led Powderly down the steps, Detective Quinones came over to Nancy and Detective Hawkins. "You okay, Hawk?" he asked, helping the detective to his feet.

Hawkins nodded. "I feel pretty dumb, though. I mean, to think I believed Stan when he said he wanted my car last night because his was in the shop. I had no idea he was setting me up. I thought the guy was my friend!"

Quinones ran his fingers through his hair. "If it helps any, it seems as though he had everyone fooled."

Shaking his head ruefully, Hawkins said, "That's for sure. When I drove up, Stan waved me into R. H. Shipping and took me up here to show me the chop shop. I was thinking what a great bust, when *wham!* He must've hit me on the head with something hard." He rubbed the back of his neck.

"You need to take it easy," Quinones told him. "The medics will be here any minute."

Nancy took the tape recorder from her pocket and handed it to Detective Quinones. "It's all on here," she said.

"Hey, Hawk!" Officer Jackson called from the top of the steps. "The dispatcher just called. You're to meet your wife at the hospital. Seems you're going to be a dad!"

"All right!" B.D. whooped. "Baby number four. I've been moonlighting as a security guard to make enough money for a down payment on a bigger house. We've kind of grown out of the old place."

Quinones burst out laughing. "So *that's* why

you've been so tense and edgy and hard to get in touch with. And all this time I thought it was because you were being paid off by car thieves."

"Sorry I didn't tell you about the moonlighting," said B.D. "I was afraid you'd make me quit. The only person I did tell was Stan."

"Who used the information to make you look even more guilty," Nancy put in.

B.D. started for the stairs, then paused and smiled back at Nancy. "Hey, you were good back there," he said. "Ever think of joining the police force?"

"No way. It's too dangerous," she said, laughing.

"I'll be back up as soon as the medics take B.D. to the hospital," Quinones told the teens. He disappeared down the steps after Detective Hawkins.

Nancy was smiling to herself when she turned back to Bess and Dirk. They were picking through the piles of car parts. "What are you guys looking for?" Nancy asked.

"Any sign of Bess's Camaro," Dirk answered. "She's really down."

As Bess went over to peer in the window of the red sports car, Nancy noticed that it was a Camaro. It looked like the same model Bess's had been.

"Don't worry," Nancy said, going over to her friend. "When you get your insurance money, we'll just have to hunt for a car like this."

"Only it won't be the same," Bess said with a sigh. "Your first car is like your first love—you never forget it."

Nancy opened the car door. "Come on, get in. We'll go for an imaginary ride—to check out guys at The Scene."

"Oh, all right." Bess had to smile. She climbed into the driver's seat while Nancy got in the passenger side.

"This is some interior," Nancy commented, running her hands down the white leather seats. "They must've been sending this car to somebody willing to lay out big bucks."

"That's for sure," Bess agreed. "Only I don't think it was quite ready to go. Look at this ugly brown carpet."

Bess bent down and patted the floor. For a second, she was quiet, then Nancy heard her whisper, "Hey, Nan, do you smell something?"

Nancy sniffed the air. "Yeah. Car paint."

"No. I mean, down here on the floor."

Nancy leaned over and sniffed. "Your perfume."

"That's what I'm talking about!" Bess's voice rose to an excited squeal. "I'm not wearing any. The smell is coming from the carpet!"

She sat up and grabbed Nancy's hand. "Nancy, this beautiful red Camaro with white leather seats *is* my car! Remember when I spilled the perfume in it?"

Nancy's mouth fell open. "That's right!"

Just then Dirk came over carrying a huge dashboard. "Hey, Bess, do you have your VIN? This is from a Camaro, and I want to check and see if it came from yours."

While Bess rummaged through her wallet, Nancy told Dirk about the spilled perfume.

"I've heard of lots of strange ways to ID a car, but this is definitely the strangest," he said with a laugh. Taking the slip of paper Bess handed him, he added, "Now, if we can prove that this dashboard is yours *and* that it originally came from this now-red Camaro, then even the police will have to be convinced."

Bess leaned forward and hugged the Camaro's steering wheel. "I just know this car is mine." Then she sat back with a serious expression. "Only when I get it back, I'm definitely equipping it with some antitheft devices!"

The next day Nancy, Bess, and Dirk were at the drag strip huddled around Big D's Dynomite.

"Well, your Camaro may have gotten a facelift," Dirk said to Bess, "but I'm afraid the Big D won't be ready in time for the Memorial Day race."

Bess squeezed his hand. "I'm really sorry."

Giving Bess a quick kiss on the cheek, he said, "At least everything else turned out okay. The notorious River Heights chop shop will soon be an empty warehouse."

"And since Kitty turned herself in and is

testifying against Powderly, he'll be in jail for a long, long time," Nancy added.

"Jake went over to post Kitty's bail this morning," Dirk told the girls. "They should be here any minute."

A few minutes later Nancy saw Jake and Kitty walking through the entrance to the pit area. The two were holding hands and beaming at each other.

"Hey! We've got good news," Jake said as the couple came up to the Big D. "Since Kitty's providing testimony that will put Stan Powderly behind bars, Detective Quinones is going to speak to the judge about giving her a suspended sentence."

"I just may get probation," Kitty said hopefully.

Jake looked down at her with a serious expression. "A *long* probation where you won't be able to get even a speeding ticket."

"That's okay," said Kitty. "I'm just happy for a second chance. I'm never going to break the law again. After all, it cost me my brother." Turning to Nancy, she added, "I can't thank you enough. If it wasn't for you and Bess, I'd be running for my life."

"It was your information that helped close up the chop shop," Bess told Kitty.

Kitty nodded. "I'm glad of that. From now on, I'll earn the money needed to race Jimmy's dream car by being the best mechanic on the drag strip."

"Well, I'm definitely going to need a mechanic to help get the Big D back in shape," Dirk said with a sigh.

"Thanks," Kitty told him. She and Jake exchanged a grin, and Kitty said, "Do you want to tell him, Jake?"

"Tell me what?" Dirk asked.

Jake grinned and slapped Dirk on the shoulder. "Kitty's going to need someone to drive Jimmy's car in the Memorial Day race. How about it?"

Dirk's mouth fell open, and Bess jumped up and gave him a hug. "Say yes!" she urged.

"Yes!" Dirk cried, throwing his baseball cap in the air. Laughing, Nancy picked it up from the ground and plopped it back on his head.

With a huge grin, Dirk slid his arms around Bess's and Nancy's shoulders. "Definitely yes. And with Nancy and Bess crewing for me, I'm bound to win!"

Nancy's next case:

Nancy, Bess, and George are off on a continental adventure into the gorgeous heart of Europe: Switzerland. And gorgeous is just the word for jet-setter Franz Haussman, who invites the girls out for a night of dancing at a chic club on the shores of Lake Geneva. But before the music ends, the mystery begins . . . and Franz's life hangs in the balance!

Soon after Franz receives a death threat, Nancy finds herself in the eye of an Alpine storm of romantic intrigue, family scandal, and big-business blackmail. Nancy's summer abroad is just getting started, but Franz draws her into a world of jealousy, ambition, and greed as dark and twisting as the medieval streets of old-town Geneva . . . in *SWISS SECRETS,* Case #72 in the Nancy Drew Files™ and the first book in the Passport to Romance trilogy.